THE FINAL EXAM

SKYE WARREN

CHAPTER ONE

That Fancy School

WHAT HAPPENS WHEN your world falls apart?

How do you go on living?

As it turns out, the answer is easy. The heart keeps on beating. The brain keeps sending out electrical impulses. It feels like there's a gaping hole in my chest, but when I look in the mirror, I'm still ordinary Anne Hill with red-rimmed eyes from crying.

When you're young and bold, full of invincibility, it's easy to decry Juliet's actions. So what if your lover is dead? To kill yourself is weak and pointless. That's what people say, but have they done it? Have they held the man they loved and felt his life slip away?

Because the pain is worse than death.

Unfortunately, I'm too well versed in survival.

After his death, Daisy worried over me like a

mother hen. No chick was ever so closely watched. Professor Avery Miller even arranged for me to visit a therapist at the university's health services. Apparently I'm supposed to give myself time to mourn. So it's convenient that I have an entire summer I can devote to the process.

From my bedroom, I can hear the not-so-muffled sound of my parents fighting.

"Did you spend all our money on your whores?"

"You're fucking insane, woman. I spend all my time taking care of you. When would I have time to visit the whores?"

"Yeah, and I notice that you didn't deny it."

"Maybe I *should* go see a whore. Someone who isn't as crazy as you."

I'm lying on my old twin bed, body flat, arms crossed over my middle. Almost as if I'm lying in a grave. Morbid thoughts for a morbid summer. After all, I can still feel the sticky residue of blood on my hands. I can still feel the hot life force of Professor William Stratford leaving his body, only cool emptiness behind.

More screams, a higher pitch. "I hate you."

"Good. I hate you, too. I should walk out and let you die."

"Do it."

"I might."

"I wish *you* were dead."

The only warmth anywhere comes from Rusty, who's curled up at my feet. I think he uses my room as a sanctuary when I'm at school. That's a small comfort for me. It hurts to abandon him every time I leave, to see more white hair in his soulful face each time I come back.

Escaping is a solo activity.

If I tried to bring the world with me, I'd have no chance. Then again, I'm back in my old room, feeling as helpless as if I were twelve, so it didn't work that well anyway.

A sharp shriek, and then a crash.

There's a formula to things, even things like a daily screaming match.

This is about the time it gets violent.

When I was very small, I would run out to try and protect my mother. Even though she'd been the one to start throwing things, more likely than not. My father always took the bait. He hit her, knocking her over, bruising her. Making her sicker, which for some reason, some mental instability, she wanted to be.

Strange, how life was always so happy to illuminate things for you. It had seemed perverse, before, the idea that my mother might want, *need* to be sick. But now I want it, too. To make my body match the acid-fire pain of my soul.

When I defended her, I usually ended up slapped or cuffed on the side of the head. Or, once, I was stomped on. Couldn't use my left hand for a month.

They didn't want my interference.

And I'm too tired to give it now.

I force my aching joints into motion, like cranking a heavy, rusted moat, the chains clinking down, providing a path forward. I climb out the window, the way I've done a million times before. My bike has carried me up and down Port Lavaca. Olde Faithful. That's what I would call it if I gave it a name.

It carries me now toward the town proper. I pass the diner where I've worked many a shift. They expected me back this summer, but I didn't start work. It was a fleeting pleasure, confounding my parents that way. They've always taken money I've made. And I've always been willing to work. It confused the hell out of them, them wanting money when they know I don't have any.

Instead I ride to my favorite place in the whole world.

The Port Lavaca Library.

It's in an unassuming, squat building. I've

heard it used to be the police station, which is a grim beginning for a place of wonder. And a notable commentary on our society, that learning should get the cast-offs of armed men, while they move somewhere nicer.

Doesn't matter.

Even with its drab countenance, I still found refuge inside.

"There you are." Ms. O'Connor pokes her head above the waist-height shelves in the children's section. She has a clear basket of picture books propped on her hip, the same way a woman of the old farming days might carry around vegetables. "I was wondering when you'd remember to read a book. Kids these days, so focused on video games."

She's being funny, but it's too hard for me to crack a smile.

Her face falls. "Your parents?"

A shrug. "They're the same as ever."

Dark eyes scan me from head to toe. "Are you hurt?"

"No, I stayed out of trouble."

"Double, double toil and trouble," she says. "Fire burn, and cauldron bubble."

Half of what she says is in Shakespeare. I understood the meaning before I'd ever cracked a play open. She's the reason I even wanted to read them. It wasn't in ninth grade literature that I first read *Romeo and Juliet*. It was Ms. O'Connor, telling me to *deny thy father and refuse thy name.* It was her telling me, *thou art thyself, though not a Hill.*

I wasn't my family. I didn't have to become them.

That was the promise slipped into the dusty pages of books.

She checked them out to me in tidy piles, week after week, telling me that I could be something more than a diner waitress. The lesson finally stuck, because I'm not working this summer. No reason to.

Books, books, money for books.

That was the excuse I gave myself for working so hard, even if the money went to my mother's unnecessary medicine for made-up illnesses.

I don't need money right now.

Because here, in the library, there is an oasis of free books.

"You're sad," she says. "Something is wrong."

The man I love died. Do you have a Shakespeare quote for that? "I'm fine."

She sighs. "You lie to me, like usual. At least I don't see any bruises on your face. At least you aren't walking funny, limping, holding your arms to the side."

I used to beg her not to tell anyone.

She didn't listen, of course. She told the police in town.

They visited our house once, during which my parents were shocked, appalled, hurt at the idea that they would ever hurt their daughter.

Then she told the social services in Tanglewood, seeing as how Port Lavaca doesn't have them. Jurisdiction, they said. They couldn't help.

And so she resorted to such things as bandages and Advil, her eyes furious but her hands gentle as she tended to me. It felt good to have someone who cared enough to do that.

William cared enough to do that.

Heat presses against my closed eyelids. I can't let myself think about him.

"Did you ever love someone?" The words spill out of me.

Pages rustle. There's a particular sound to the thick protective covers she puts on the books here. I've helped her do it, wiping down a new book and then carefully, carefully gluing down a clear coat, making the books last longer.

Ms. O'Connor stands from her rummage, producing a thin volume.

Macbeth.

My eyebrows rise. That's an unconventional answer, but then Ms. O'Connor is an unconventional person. "Yes," she says. "Of course I've been in love. You can't help it, you know. It would be like trying to outrun a storm."

I blink fast, eyes wide, trying to dry out the tears. "In that case, I got drenched."

"Good," she says, her voice gentle. "That's more important than books. In fact, it's the reason for them. Shakespeare, or whoever wrote those plays, didn't write about love so that you wouldn't have to live it. They wrote to put words to the inevitable pain of it, so you would know what to call it."

"At least you admit he wrote them," I say, an attempt at misdirection.

It's an old argument, one that never fails to make her smile. "What do they teach you at that fancy school of yours?"

"Mostly they're purists."

"Of course they are," she says, her tone gently mocking. "It's a form of worship. The Bard as scholastic god. They would probably excommunicate anyone who said otherwise."

Purists are the people who believe that Shakespeare himself wrote every word of every iamb, pen to parchment. However, most plays at that time were written by entire troupes, collaborations that were unconcerned with the individual.

Shakespeare himself never published a single piece of work with his own name on it, lending credence to the idea that he knew they weren't his own. In fact, even purists must acknowledge that he borrowed heavily, sometimes even word-for-word, from source plays and other works.

I have always been a purist.

Maybe I needed a god to believe in.

She pushes the book across the counter to me. *Macbeth*. "I'll scan this for you. It will give you something to read for the rest of the summer."

My eyebrows draw together. Here is a play that has little to do with love. Instead, there is ambition and violence. And witches, of course. Three witches with omens that aren't to be trusted, somehow. Even though they also come true. "This isn't one of my favorites."

"No," she says, agreeing with me. "You liked the stories of strong women, even if Shakespeare didn't give them full thrift. You liked arguing for them, and you're damned good at it."

"If I don't do it, who will?"

"I think fancy schools aren't kind to women, either."

Kind? No. I was basically run out of town, under accusations of sleeping my way to the top, of letting a professor write my paper for me. Of trading my body for an academic award.

A tear slips down my cheek.

Never mind that I earned it fair and square.

Never mind that the man who supposedly wrote it is dead.

Never mind that my heart is broken.

The scanner makes a familiar beep as it runs over the barcode. "Take it."

I sigh. "Really?"

She taps the cover, which depicts a bloody crown. "You can't always argue for the best possible interpretation. Sometimes people are just wrong. Sometimes they're just cruel. That's the part of Shakespeare you never wanted to face."

Before I can think of a response, she says, "Hold, please."

She hurries back at the strange sound, almost like liquid, a stream of it.

There should never be liquid in a library.

I wince at the sound of Ms. O'Connor's exasperated sigh from the back of the library. "Sir, please. The restroom is right over there." She's dealing with a man who's clearly had too much to drink, judging by the slurred responses and the unmistakable sound of a zipper. I should probably help her, but my feet remain rooted to the spot.

I've seen enough nastiness in my life. I don't need to clean up someone else's mess. Not today.

I run my fingers over the glossy cover of *Macbeth*, tracing the embossed title. There was a time when I thought being a librarian was the most magical job in the world. Surrounded by books all day, helping people find the right story to lose themselves in. But Ms. O'Connor showed me that a librarian is so much more than a keeper of books. She's a social worker, a nurse, a teacher, a confidante. She's the heart of this community, and she gives so much of herself to keep it beating.

I admire her for it, but I know myself well enough to know that I can't be that selfless. I've given too much of myself already, to parents who took and took without ever giving back. I needed a place where I can be selfish, where I could lose myself in the pages of a book and not worry about anyone else's needs.

Books never ask for anything.

They offer up their pages, day after day, providing escape, providing answers. I flip open *Macbeth* and read the opening scene. The three witches, the weird sisters, huddled together, plotting and scheming.

When shall we three meet again?

I glance around, waiting for Ms. O'Connor to return.

A young girl, maybe eight or nine, wearing a black cape that's frayed at the edges, a Styrofoam sword leaning against her chair. She's hunched over one of the library's ancient computers, her small hands gripping the mouse tightly. Her brow is furrowed in concentration, eyes narrowed at the screen.

She glances at me briefly, her scowl deepening, before turning back to her game. Her character, a princess in a purple dress, falls off a cliff and disappears into a pit of lava. The screen flashes red, the level restarts.

I don't know her name.

Even though I used to know everyone in this town.

The years that I've been gone have changed me.

It's a surprise to find that the town has changed, too.

I wander closer so I can watch as she moves through it again, this time trying to press the right vocabulary words faster so that the princess avoids the dungeon. I must have spent hours, days, weeks of my life playing Lanternleaf Legends.

The game is heavily pixelated and laggy. Old.

Still good, though. Still useful.

I don't help her with the vocabulary, but when she hesitates at the entrance, I help her out. "There's an ogre in there."

"I know," she snaps, even though it's clear she didn't.

Her princess runs, teeters on the edge of the cliff, then leaps, soaring over the lava and landing safely on the other side. She doesn't smile, but her shoulders relax slightly. We watch the little show in which the princess is crowned, allowed to pass into the next level, this one harder of course.

It's a strange prize, the option to face an even stronger foe.

A compelling one.

The girl has a scowl on her small face. Her bad mood serves as a shield. It keeps other people away. Only now, with grown-up eyes, I can see the pain underneath. I can see the loneliness that safety creates.

I used to come here all the time when I was her age.

Possibly Ms. O'Connor bandages her, too.

My heart aches for her, and for the memories she stirs, memories of a little girl hiding in the library, finding solace in learning, trying to escape the nightmare of home.

I'm not sure I've ever really escaped.

The worn copy of *Macbeth* doesn't give me the stir of excitement I normally have with Shakespeare. Then again, I'm not sure any of them would help. My drive is gone. I'm not sure how pages and pages of mindless, gory ambition will help. I've already seen first-hand what ruthless schemes create.

What do they teach you at that fancy school of yours?

Tanglewood University taught me Shakespeare thoroughly.

They taught it by having me live it.

I flip through the graying pages. Someone left notes in the margin. Another person drew what appears to be a penis on the inside cover. Ms. O'Connor didn't catch that when it was returned. She would have used her trusty bottle of white-out to remove the offending ink.

They would probably excommunicate anyone who said otherwise.

Maybe I can use the religious fervor for a purpose.

For revenge.

Ms. O'Connor didn't give me something to read this summer.

She gave me something to write.

CHAPTER TWO

The Scottish Play

B IRDS SING OUTSIDE the window. There's something wise about animals, the way they aren't affected by human dramas.

I squeeze my eyes tight. It does nothing to block the cheery sound, of course. I've always loved their morning music, a much gentler alarm than the one on my phone. It's only now that I'm torn by grief that I wish I didn't have to hear them sing. I'm back at Tanglewood University. Back in my dorm room.

It doesn't feel the same. I'm sure it never will.

I burrow deeper into the blanket, seeking warmth, seeking comfort.

Seeking something that isn't here.

The other side of the room is a mirror image of mine. Daisy's bed is neatly made, her desk organized. She's an early riser, something I've always envied. At the moment, I'm grateful to have a moment to collect myself.

Whispers from outside the door.

That means I should wake up. My feet hit the creaky wood floor.

A small mirror is taped to the inside of the door. It reflects back dull brown eyes, limp brown hair. I look as desolate as I feel. I can't help but think of another pair of dark, mysterious eyes that looked at me with such intensity.

He's gone now, along with any hope I had.

Along with any hope the university had, for that matter.

Daisy bursts into the room, a whirlwind of blonde hair and a big smile. She's holding a glass of orange juice and a plate of scrambled eggs.

"Don't argue," she says, her voice singsong. "I knew you wouldn't eat if I left you to your own devices."

I recognize the stained plastic of the cup and army-green color of the plate. "They let you take those out of the cafeteria?"

"No one can argue with me when I'm on a mission."

That much I can believe. She has these hopeful blue eyes that make you want to promise her a pony and world peace.

It's what obliges me to sit down and force the

food into my mouth, even though it tastes like sawdust. That's not the grief talking. Hathaway cafeteria food always tastes like sawdust.

She packs her backpack while I eat, keeping one eye on me. "I was worried I'd have to wake you up or you'd be late for class."

"It would be better if I did."

"What are you talking about?"

"It doesn't matter. Nothing does."

"He would want you to go."

Would he? I'm not sure about that, not knowing who's running it. Though his wishes don't really get to factor in right now. That's what happens when you die. You stop getting a say. I turn away from her, looking out the small window. "I'm not sure I can face them."

There's silence for a moment, then Daisy stands up and walks over to me. She places a hand on my shoulder, her touch comforting. "I know you're hurting. I'm here for you. Just don't make any rash decisions, okay?"

I look at her, at the sincerity in her eyes, and a lump forms in my throat. I swallow it down, forcing a smile. "I'm fine."

She doesn't believe me.

And why should she? I don't even believe myself.

I am a train wreck. Not hypothetically. I'm a train wreck that makes everyone crane their necks, even the nicest people driven to gawk as I leave the dorm and cross the campus.

Daisy does her part as my best friend to glare at everyone.

It helps, but she can't follow me around all day.

For example, she can't follow me to *Advanced Shakespeare: Violence, Fate, and Revolution*. It's taught by Professor Isolde Thorne. There aren't any other options if I'm going to graduate this year. She controls the entire freaking department now, thanks to her alliance with Luca Andini.

I step into the lecture hall, leaving the chill from the drafty hallway and entering a dry sauna of an old radiator. The room has curved rows of old-fashioned wooden desks, each with a tiny desk attached. Tall, narrow windows line the walls, filtering in light through yellowed panes.

Professor Thorne stands at the front of the room, her elegant figure silhouetted against the chalkboard. She's writing something, her handwriting sharp and precise.

The Scottish Play, it says.

I want to run up to her, to shake her, to accuse her of murder.

Instead I avert my gaze and force myself to find an empty desk in the back row. The desk creaks as I sit down, the sound echoing in the quiet room. I look around, taking in the other students. They're all familiar faces, fellow literature majors I've shared classes with since freshman year.

The usual pre-class chatter is subdued.

They may not know the details of the Shakespeare Society, but they know that a dark cloud has settled over the department. Everyone feels it, their shoulders hunched, their eyes downcast as they wait for class to begin.

My notebook is filled with scribbled notes from old classes and late-night thoughts during study sessions from last year.

I can't imagine writing a single thing.

Can't imagine caring enough.

Thorne turns around, her eyes scanning the room. They land on me, and for a moment, we lock gazes. I see the challenge in her gaze, the silent dare.

Unlike the other people here, I *do* know the details.

Which means I'm a threat, an obstacle in her quest for total power.

I refuse to be intimidated. Refuse to let her see

the pain inside me. I'm the little girl in the library again, raising my chin, taking on the entire world rather than admit that it hurt me.

She smiles, as if pleased.

That's not a good sign.

"Welcome, students," she says, "to the most important class of your undergraduate tenure. This is the class that decides whether you graduate with a degree from our esteemed fine arts program or whether you flunk out in your final year."

A murmur ripples through the lecture hall, a mix of nervous laughter and whispered anxieties. Bile rises in my throat. The only reason to keep attending this year is so that I can graduate, but it may not matter.

Thorne hates me enough to fail me no matter what I turn in.

"Half of your grade will be from assignments in class. And the other half is from your final exam. I won't go easy on you. It will be the hardest thing you've ever done. Only students with the best papers will make it through."

There's no laughter this time, nervous or otherwise.

They know she's dead serious.

"I have an offering for you. A gift. I'll tell you what the final exam will be right now, on the first day of class. You'll have an entire semester to prepare for it. Now, say *thank you*."

There are some mumbled *thank yous*.

Meanwhile, knuckles turn white from their grip on pens.

It's clear this won't be a real gift. If she's giving us an entire semester to prepare for the final exam, the expectations will be that much higher.

"Each one of you will be asked to prove—or disprove—one thing. That Shakespeare himself wrote *The Scottish Play*. You won't find out which one you get until the exam."

A few whispered exclamations. Someone gasps.

As a school steeped in traditions, Tanglewood University does not often address the question of authorship. They want us all to assume, as the world usually has, that Shakespeare wrote all the plays. We don't even bother to make the arguments, since suggesting otherwise would be blasphemous.

Even so, we'd have an edge, arguing for authorship.

It's the default assumption. The easy A.

Another student raises her hand, asking for clarification.

And Professor Thorne is pleased to give it.

Yes, it will be random which students must argue for the opposite case, that someone else wrote *Macbeth*.

Random, my ass.

I see it in her eyes—the calculation, the malice. She wants me to fail. My grade will have little to do with how I perform on the exam.

Everyone looks worried.

Tyler is here. Our eyes meet.

He turns away from me.

Apparently we're on our own this semester.

I can't blame him for wanting distance. It won't help anyone to be my friend in this class, but it still hurts to know I'm alone.

Thorne paces the length of the stage, her heels clicking against the worn wood. "Now, let's begin. *The Scottish Play* embodies the theme of violence."

Someone raises their hand, and she nods. "What is *the Scottish Play*?" they ask.

Damn. It gets quiet enough in the lecture hall that we can hear students calling to each other outside. The professor's eyes narrow. "We don't use its name."

The student looks around, wide-eyed. They know they've messed up, but it's not like they can figure it out from context clues if they haven't already.

Professor Thorne looks at me. "Perhaps you'd like to help elucidate."

She wants me to say the name. As if I can get more doomed than I already am.

"Macbeth," I say, and there's a rumble of uneasy movement throughout the room. "People say it's cursed. One time a riot began in the streets while two competing companies put on productions. In another case, supposedly, a real dagger was used instead of a stage prop. And in the original staging by Shakespeare, the actor playing Lady Macbeth died shortly after the first performance. Such a tragedy."

The last word I say with a note of irony.

Not because I'm calloused toward that long ago passing. The irony is a subtle dig at the woman standing in front of the class, the woman who has startling similarities to Lady Macbeth.

Her lips firm. She doesn't miss the accusation.

There's at least some upside to having a mortal enemy who's in Mensa.

"We don't say the name of the play," Thorne says. "Instead we call it *The Scottish Play*. All scholars know what it means. It's a sign of respect to Shakespeare, as well as the talented actors and directors. Do you respect them, Ms. Hill?"

Pretty words. I don't believe them. I think it adds a level of drama to her lecture. It adds a level of performance, because that's what this is. She's not interested in teaching.

She's interested in being admired and feared.

"I'm not superstitious, if that's what you're asking."

"So you don't believe the play is cursed?"

"I don't believe that witches got angry because Shakespeare used lines for a real curse, because I don't believe that curses are real. Humans cause enough evil without magic."

Her lids drop. "Since you brought her up, let's talk about Lady Macbeth."

"So we can say the character's name but not the title of the play?" someone asks.

Thorne's eyes flash. "You may leave the class if you wish to shout like a baboon."

The person shrinks in their seat.

She continues serenely. "Death, blood, gore. Their purpose, of course, is symbolic. Consider Lady Macbeth's obsession with cleanliness. What does it symbolize?"

"OCD," someone says, which sets off a round of snickers.

"Regret." Someone else. "It represents the blood on her hands."

Her eyes meet mine.

I'm not afraid of her. I raise my hand, meeting her gaze head-on.

She narrows her eyes. "Yes?"

Well, maybe I *am* afraid of her, but I'm not going to let that stop me. "It's irony. She wants to spurn motherhood and femininity, and yet she's chained herself to the historically feminine task of cleaning."

"So, you suggest she cannot get free from gendered expectations?"

I take a deep breath. "Exactly. The same way that some women claim to be interested in merit, in achievement, but they actually get what they want by pandering to men."

Someone gasps. Yes, that was blatant, wasn't it? I'm proud of myself for saying it, for making the accusation in full view of her students.

She raises a penciled brow. "That's an interesting claim coming from you. Do you have personal experience with pandering to powerful men?"

I should probably be cowering, ashamed that I had sex with my professor.

Except it didn't give me anything.

It never would have given me anything except for scorn.

I would have had to play the game to do that,

to wheedle him for favors, to suck his cock so he'd write my papers. I would have had to do what Thorne herself does, aligning herself to Andini. "I've seen it happen right in front of my eyes, a woman urging a man to violence. It doesn't lead anywhere pretty."

Her lids drop. This is a woman who thrives on her looks.

It's a very specific kind of beauty. Her pencil skirt makes it clear that she's sexual. Her white Oxford shirt, buttoned all the way up, proclaims her intelligence. Her red lipstick makes it clear that you'll listen to her, whether you like it or not—though you'll probably like it.

She wouldn't want me insulting such a careful aesthetic.

It's a costume, really, like any actor would wear.

"Violence," she says. "It's an interesting idea for a woman. We have less strength, don't we? Less physical strength, usually. And yet Lady Macbeth became the queen of Scotland without ever lifting a sword."

"Power," I say. "Strength. Violence. Those are just tools. The play is about ambition. It's about the bloody ends that come to those who are slaves to it."

CHAPTER THREE

Inside The Globe

THORNE IGNORES ME for the rest of class.

It's a small blessing.

Class eventually ends with the harsh scrape of chairs against the worn floor. Students gather their belongings, eager to escape.

I take my time, deliberately slow as I pack my notebook and pens into my bag. My heart hammers in my chest, anticipation coursing through my veins.

Most of the students have already filed out, their voices echoing down the hallway. Thorne is at the front of the room, watching.

Good.

I reach into my bag, pulling out the decoy—a battered manuscript, the paper yellowed, ink faded. I make a show of trying to hide it, my hands fumbling as I tuck it into the inner pocket of my bag.

I stand up, slinging my bag over my shoulder.

One step toward the door.

Another.

"Ms. Hill," she calls out, her voice sharp. I freeze, like a deer caught in headlights. Her gaze flicks to my bag, then back to me. She knows. "A moment, please."

"Yes, Professor Thorne?"

She walks toward me, her heels clicking against the floor. Her eyes never leave mine, her gaze intense, probing. She stops in front of me, her hand outstretched. "What's in your bag?"

I clutch my bag tighter, my knuckles turning white. "Nothing."

Thorne's lips thin. "Don't lie to me."

I take a deep breath, my heart pounding in my ears. I reach into my bag, my hand wrapping around the pages. I pull them out, my hand trembling slightly. Thorne's eyes widen in surprise as she takes in the battered appearance.

She snatches it from me, her fingers brushing against mine.

I suppress a shudder at the contact.

The old script is convincing. "What is this?"

"It was a gift. From Professor Stratford. It's mine."

Thorne's grip tightens on it, her knuckles

turning white. She knows the significance, if it ever belonged to Stratford. "It looks old. And valuable. I don't think he gave it to you. I think you stole it from him."

My heart races. "I did not."

"Perhaps I should take this to the ethics office."

I look up at her, my eyes filling with tears. They aren't fake tears, but I'm not crying for the reason she thinks. "I didn't steal it. I was working on it with him, when he…when he died. Writing notes for him. That's all."

Thorne's eyes flash, a mixture of anger and triumph. She thinks she's won, thinks she's broken me. "I understand. And you probably didn't know who to return it to, after his untimely passing."

"Yes," I say, sounding grateful.

She tucks the book under her arm, her eyes never leaving mine. "Don't worry, Ms. Hill. You aren't in trouble. The university owns whatever he was working on, which means the university now owns this manuscript. Your help, such as it is, will no longer be needed."

I nod, pretending to be upset. "I understand."

She turns away, dismissing me. I watch as she walks back to her desk, the pages still tucked under her arm. I can see the tension in her shoulders, the rigid set of her back. She's excited.

I turn around, my heart pounding in my chest. I've planted the seed of revenge. Whether it will come to anything, I don't know, but I walk out of the lecture hall wearing a small smile.

The smile doesn't last for long.

The courtyard outside the building is usually full of students on their way to class. A few of them might lounge on the grass studying. Or a couple of jocks might roughhouse.

Today everyone has their heads together, whispering, gossiping. News of the liberal arts department has never been this scandalous before.

And Brandon stands at the coffee shop.

It's shocking how much he looks like his father. I didn't see the resemblance the first time I met Professor Stratford at the Pinnacle Hotel. That's because he's the original, the fully formed version. While Brandon has softer edges, as if he's still growing into his face. I'd found him cute once.

Now I find him heartbreaking. He reminds me of what's gone.

He straightens when he sees me, as if he's been waiting for me.

That's not what I need today.

I try to avoid him, but he steps in front of me, holding out a steaming paper cup. "The way you like it," he says.

Damn it. I do want caffeine, but I don't want it to be from him. I'm not even sure what it's supposed to be. A peace offering? A bribe? "No, thanks."

I don't stop walking, but he doesn't take the hint.

Instead, he follows me as I head toward my next class.

A girl whispers to her friend as I walk by. Her eyes dart to me, then quickly away. Her friend nods, her brows furrowed.

I quicken my pace, eager to escape. The murmurs grow louder as I pass.

"Go away," I mutter. "Or we're both going to end up on Tanglewood Tea."

"So what?"

I make a sound like a growl. It's what comes out naturally as I hold my hand out for the coffee, muttering a surly *thanks*. "Maybe you don't care about everyone gossiping about you, but I do."

"They don't even know what they're talking about."

"That doesn't stop them."

He sighs. "Maybe we can talk about this in

private?"

That makes me stop. He's sighing at me, as if I'm the annoying one? "What does that even mean? Like should we go have dinner somewhere, maybe head to the pub for a few drinks with your frat-boy friends?"

An uneasy shift. "It doesn't have to be like that."

"What would it be like, then?" I can tell my voice is rising, but I can't seem to soften it. It's either yell at my ex-boyfriend or start sobbing in the middle of campus. "Would it be a date? Now that your dad is dead we can have sex again?"

He flinches. Everyone is listening now, watching us.

I take a deep breath. "I'm sorry. I know you lost your father. I know you're grieving, but I'm not going to be the one to comfort you through it."

"I know that."

"Then what do you want from me?"

He runs a hand through his hair, a nervous gesture I remember all too well. His father has a similar one. Had a similar one. I have to remember he's in the past tense now. "I don't know."

"Once you figure it out, maybe you can explain it to me. All I know is that Professor

Stratford is dead, and you wouldn't even let me grieve him."

That was the only text I had sent, a month after school let out. I asked where he'd been buried. It's not like I was going to stroll through the funeral or anything. I only wanted to lay flowers there. And maybe a book.

He'd left me on read. Unanswered.

"Anne, please. It's complicated."

"Yes, it's complicated. And every single version leads to one thing: I should be allowed to mourn him. I should be allowed to stand by his grave with flowers. So if I'm not even good enough for that, then you can go to hell."

A feminine voice rings out. "Anne!"

My friend Carlisle pushes her way through the crowd. Her pretty face is marred with worry. "What's going on? Is he bothering you?"

I brush tears away from my eyes. "It's fine. I was just leaving."

Her soulful eyes search me. Then she loops her arm through mine, helping me escape the crowd. I let her lead me away, grateful for her help. The stares follow me like a shadow.

I take a deep breath, trying to rein in my emotions.

The chatter fades into the background, replaced by the crunch of gravel under our feet. The air is crisp, the sun casting a warm glow over the campus, a stark contrast to the grief coiled within me.

"You okay?" Carlisle asks, her voice soft.

"I'm fine. Just…frustrated. Everyone saw me talking to him. That is probably going to end up on Tanglewood Tea."

She squeezes my arm, her grip reassuring. "No, it won't."

I manage a small smile, grateful for her support even though I don't believe her. "They've been posting a lot about Thorne and the takeover. They're hinting at some pretty dark stuff. Stuff about the Shakespeare Society too."

Carlisle's grip on my arm tightens. "That's a good thing, right?"

"Sure. It's good. A little late, though."

She's silent, her gaze fixed on the path ahead. "Late?"

"Late, now that he's dead. They're the ones who outed my relationship with him. Maybe he would still be alive if not for that."

"Do you really think that?"

"I don't know, but if they talk shit about me, then I won't be safe either."

She stops and faces me. "They never mentioned your name."

I frown, remembering. It's a little hazy in the miasma of grief, but she's right. They only said that Professor Stratford was sleeping with a student. It was the student doing work-study in the office that handed out our mentorship assignments who shared my name. "Why are you defending them?"

She bites her lip. "I'm not."

Shit. I made her feel bad. I didn't mean to do that. "Listen, I'm sorry."

"God, don't apologize."

"No, I need to. You were so great coming to my rescue back there. I'm not great company right now."

Her eyes turn almost watery. "Anne."

She can't start crying. If she does, then I'll start crying. And if I start crying, I'll never stop. "I've got to go, okay?"

I head for the library, my throat tight, my shoulders down.

Over the summer, I read every article I could find that touched on Professor Stratford's death. The official label was a heart attack, so there's no discussion of poison or murder. Each one felt like a slap in the face. Still, I read them because I hoped that one of them would have found out where he was buried. It only occurs to me now that I have another resource.

The grand entrance of the Registrar's Office looms before me, its heavy glass doors revealing desks. It also contains the Hall of Faculty. That's a fancy name for a dusty corner on the second floor. It contains the name of every professor who's ever taught at Tanglewood University.

Which means he should be there.

Along with the date of his death…and the location of his grave.

Some famous people have graduated from this university. Their photos are framed on the wall, some even signed. Actors, judges, politicians, CEOs, poets. I find the little box labeled *S*, then the index paper that says *Stratford, William*. It has his degrees, his honors, professional publications. There's even a section for some documentaries he's in, such as *Inside the Globe: Hidden Secrets Inside Shakespeare's Theater*. I'll have to look it up online, even though it will be heartbreaking to see him.

Under death, it has this year.

And nothing else.

Where the place of burial would be, it's blank.

CHAPTER FOUR

The Dead Sea

'M IN PROFESSOR Stratford's office, the rich scent of old books and leather surrounding me. He's rolling up his sleeves, revealing strong forearms. Reading, of course, in a leather chair, by the light of a green banker's lamp.

He looks up when I step inside.

"Anne," he murmurs, his voice a low rumble.

He's holding me.

Space and time mean nothing here.

Death has no power.

His fingers trace the line of my jaw, tilting my face up to his. His lips capture mine, hungry and demanding. I melt into him, my body pressing against his. He tastes like whiskey and desire, a heady mix that goes straight to my head.

His hands roam my body, possessive, knowing exactly what they want. He cups my breast, his thumb brushing over my nipple through the thin fabric of my shirt. I gasp into his mouth, feeling a rush of heat between my legs. He growls in response, deepening the kiss.

"I've missed you," he says, his voice rough. His hand slides down to my hip, pulling me against him. I can feel his arousal, his hard cock. It's ready for me, and God, my body is ready too—slick and hot and squeezing.

Then I wake up, gasping.

A dream. It was only a dream.

The orange light through the window makes me blink in confusion. I'm not really someone who naps, but I fell into bed after classes. I've had enough of Thorne's sly smiles. I've had enough of whispers on campus.

It's exhausting.

Grief is exhausting.

I'm learning to hate Professor Stratford. It's not fair to feel that way about someone who can't defend themself, but I can't help it. He shouldn't have made me fall for him. He shouldn't have made life seem beautiful.

I was happy enough with survival. Before him.

A knock startles me.

Is it Lorelei complaining that we left towels on the floor of the bathroom again? I open the door, my eyes widening as I take in the sight of

Professor Avery Miller, professor of ancient history. Her beauty and poise look out of place in the slouched, pock-marked hallway of Hathaway Dormitory.

She smiles. "Hello, Anne."

"Um." I glance behind me. No answers there. "Hi?"

"I know this is last minute and you might have plans already, but I was wondering if you would have dinner with me."

Plans? I don't make plans for dinner. That would require a social life. I have only a handful of friends…and my books. I glance down at my jeans and an old T-shirt from my high school debate team. Then I look at her.

She's wearing some kind of T-shirt dress that I suppose might pass for casual if you're wealthy and gorgeous. The plum color sets off her dark blonde hair. A wide sash made from the same smooth cotton ties a bow around her slender waist.

"We can go out, if you'd like," she says, since I'm standing there gawking.

"Oh, I don't know." I don't have money. I'm guessing she would pay for my meal, but that would make me feel worse. Besides, I'm not sure what she wants with me. Nothing good. She's one of the few people who know about my affair and have been kind to me, but I also hate that she needs to. I hate that I've become a pitiable person, someone who needs help, rather than a potential scholar. "I'm kind of tired."

"That's okay," she says, gentle but persistent. "We can eat in the cafeteria downstairs. Faculty get a certain number of dorm meals."

"Are you…sure?"

"Of course."

I rub the sleep from my eyes and search for my phone, which is under my desk somehow. I barely even remember stumbling in here a couple hours ago. Daisy isn't here, which strikes me as vaguely odd.

"Professor Miller, is this some kind of vigil?"

Her eyebrows rise. "Vigil?"

"Yeah, or like, a suicide watch? Daisy isn't here, so I'm wondering if she asked you to spend time with me."

She stops walking. The hallway is small enough that the conversation feels intimate. Her gentle voice adds to it. "Are you thinking about hurting yourself, Anne?"

"No. That's what I'm saying. You don't need to waste your time with me no matter what Daisy may have said."

"Hey. Enough of that. Daisy didn't ask me to come. And most importantly, you aren't a waste of time, not to anyone, definitely not to me."

They are very nice words.

That doesn't mean that they're real.

It doesn't mean I'm not a burden.

Yes, I'd do the same for Daisy. And I'd tell her she's not a burden. I'd tell that to anyone. My deep-down secret is that I'm not like everyone else. I'm worth less. That's what growing up in a household where you have to parent your parents from the time you're old enough to walk. Managing their emotions, cleaning their house, cooking their food. And then being told what you've done isn't even good enough. I've been a burden from the moment I was born, and it's left a soot-stained stamp on my soul.

I also know that the world wants me to pretend. It wants me to smile and nod and proclaim that I'm working on self-care.

So I don't argue with Professor Miller.

"Maybe for this one meal, you can call me Avery."

I give her a sideways glance. "I'm not sure I can do that."

"You graduate next semester."

"I'm pretty sure you'll always be Professor

Miller to me."

"Hmm."

The cafeteria downstairs hasn't updated the letter board since before I moved in here. *Meatloaf and green beans,* it's said for years, layers of dust and grease coated so that they probably can't even remove the yellowed letters to tell us what's actually going to be served.

It really isn't appropriate for Professor Miller in her Anne Taylor clothes, no matter how business casual they are. But she picks up a tray and enters the line, so I follow her. Spaghetti. There's a vat of spaghetti and a rock-hard breadstick. For dessert there's watery, off-brand Jell-O.

There are not-so-subtle stares as we find seats.

For once I'm not sure whether they're gawking at me for my notoriety or at Professor Miller for eating here. I've seen some professors take quick meals at Mayfair Dormitory, where they have Mediterranean bowls and house-made ice cream. Even so, they usually only eat with each other.

"Fraternization," she murmurs with a small smile, opening the little paper packet holding the silverware. "This is very taboo of us."

She's referring to the stares. They don't seem

to bother her, but she apparently notices. "I'm sorry. I should have taken your offer to go off campus."

Her hazel eyes twinkle. "Don't apologize. Believe me, I've done far more shocking things than this."

I don't bother to hide my skepticism. "Really."

A delicate, feminine snort. "One day I'll tell you how my husband and I met. Maybe once you can call me Avery."

"It might be worth it to hear the story." From the expression on her face, it sounds like it would be a good one. Though I doubt it's as…dangerous, sexual, and forbidden as how I met Professor Stratford.

"Oh, it will be," she says. "I'll give you a little hint. There was an auction."

The word auction coming out of her bow-shaped lips makes me think of the fancy kind of auctions that rich people must have, with priceless works of art and a man holding a gavel. Then another idea occurs to me.

She isn't saying that *she* was auctioned, right?

I blink.

A slow smile curves her lips. "I'll tell you one day, when we're off campus."

Maybe she wouldn't be shocked about how I met Professor Stratford in a hotel bar, offering a night with him for money to pay for books. "I think there's more to you than meets the eye."

"Good," she says. "Appearances aren't what matter. I have many published papers and lectures exploring ancient mythology that boil down to that."

"How did you choose that area of study?"

"Oh, I didn't really. It chose me."

I think back to the afternoons I spent curled up with old books checked out from the Port Lavaca Library, making friends with Juliet, learning to fear Hamlet. Studiously avoiding Macbeth. "I understand that."

"I know you do."

It occurs to me that there may be an upside to meeting with her. "I have to ask you something. Do you know where Professor Stratford is buried?"

Her eyes shadow. "No, I'm sorry."

Damn. "It's fine."

The heat stinging my eyes calls me a liar. She's kind enough to let me wipe them away with the coarse paper napkin without comment.

She was a colleague of his. She should have been invited to the funeral, along with many other people. Why the hell is it such a secret where he's buried? I wanted to find out so that I could pay my respects, maybe find some closure. Instead it's turning into a mystery.

What if he's not buried anywhere? What if he's alive?

I shake my head, dispelling the thought. It's ridiculous. Impossible. I saw him fall. I felt him die. I squeeze my eyes shut, the memory of that night playing out behind my closed lids. The underground storm shelters, the blood.

"This is such a hard thing," Professor Miller says. "You're so young, so people may want to dismiss your grief, but it's clear that you felt deeply."

"A little too deeply."

"I'm sure it's hard for you to focus on school right now."

"Yes and no. It's distracting, at least. Being at home over the summer wasn't really better. Too much time to wonder."

"That makes sense. He would be proud of you."

"No, he wouldn't."

"No?"

"I might not even graduate."

She coughs, her eyes watering, though it's unclear whether it's from what I've said or the bite of breadstick she's just taken. Possibly she doesn't know the quantity of salt being used in this kitchen daily could re-create the Dead Sea.

"Why would you say that?"

"Because…" I glance around, although most everyone has gone back to eating. "You know who's running the department now."

"Yes."

"Well…she might not pass me."

"Pass you? She'll have to prove you deserve to fail. With your grades and your reputation with other professors, that would be hard to do."

Possible, though. Especially with her neat little trick for the final exam. I might be the only student forced to argue against Shakespeare's authorship. Which means that if she fails me, and I challenge the grade, that paper will then be judged by other Shakespearean scholars— particularly ones connected to Tanglewood University already, ones who never countenance any other idea.

I don't explain the details to Professor Miller.

Or as she's starting to be called in my own head, at least, Avery.

"I wouldn't put anything past her," I say.

After a long pause, she sighs. "You're right. It would be foolish to underestimate her. Which means you might not pass."

CHAPTER FIVE

Beware the Ides

"**Y**OU COULD TRANSFER out," Professor Miller suggests.

"My academic scholarship won't move with me to another college. And getting another one at a different school will be impossible without her recommendation."

"I see."

I don't want her pity. "Don't worry though. I shouldn't have said anything."

"If it comes to that, I'll fight for you. I'm not entirely without sway in this university. And in the city."

I don't want her to make an enemy of the Society. "Seriously, I'm fine."

Her nose scrunches. Then she sighs. "Maybe you can come study the ancient Greeks. Shakespeare was fond of referencing them, even reincarnating them for his characters."

That's what made my fake manuscript so important. There are only a handful of changes from the earliest draft of *Macbeth* available. Important changes, though. Ones that make reference to a little-known Athenian play that isn't one of the extant documents that he pulls from.

It's also one that wasn't even translated into English until after 1623, when *Macbeth* was included in the first folio publication.

In other words, this means the author of the play would have had to speak Greek, as well as have access to a library full of Greek texts that might include it. Shakespeare didn't know Greek.

The fake manuscript, if real, would have been a smoking gun. It would have been proved, definitively, that another person wrote *Macbeth*. I don't believe that Professor Thorne wants to argue against authorship. She clearly loves the establishment too much for that. But even she can't ignore such a powerful piece of evidence.

It wouldn't just make her an expert.

It would make her immortal.

And when, eventually, she publishes it, she will look like a fool.

"Ancient Greek history would be interesting," I confess. "But there's no room on my scholarship for extra semesters, either."

"Maybe I could give you the money."

Dumbfounded. That's what I feel right now. "That would be…no. Impossible."

"It could be a loan."

"I….don't know what to say. That's so generous, especially when I have no collateral, no proof at all that I would ever pay it back. But I also can't take your money." When she opens her mouth to object, I say, "It doesn't really matter, because I'm tired of college. Not the work. That part I can do. It's the politics. The viciousness."

The death.

Her hazel eyes hold sympathy, as if she heard the last unspoken word.

"I wish I could tell you that this kind of thing wouldn't happen again, but I have to be honest. The academic world is cutthroat. There have always been people trying to use the university's resources to gain power—and there probably always will be. But students like you are the lifeblood. You're the reason why we fight back."

I don't want to be the reason.

That's depressing, though, so I force the conversation back to more neutral ground, asking about Professor Miller's work and life, forcing myself to eat a quarter of the spaghetti on my plate. She tells me a few antics about her two daughters, one of whom has taken after her, she says. A bookish child. The other is more of an adventurer, a troublemaker.

"Like her father," Professor Miller says ruefully.

When we're finished with dinner, I thank her for the time. Whether or not Daisy called her, I think it was a form of vigil. Checking on the poor girl who held her professor, and her lover, in her arms when he died.

I don't want to go back up to the dorm room, where Daisy will no doubt have returned and be ready to continue the vigil. Instead I go for a walk. Later in the day, there are less people around, less stares. More students have their heads down, tired as they find their way back to their dorms.

Wind slips under my sweater, tickling my stomach.

I don't realize where I am until I notice the bronze elephant statue.

The Beckinsale Library of Natural Science.

The elevator shivers its way to the fifth floor.

Doors open, and I step into heavy silence broken only by the ticking of the woefully late wall clock. Shelves stretch up to the ceiling, filled with leather-bound tomes. I run my fingers along the spines as I walk, embossed titles rough under my fingertips. *Bump. Bump. Bump.*

It's a sensory eulogy for the man I met here again and again.

I round a corner to the table where we used to meet.

So ordinary. So life-changing.

I sink into one of the chairs, the cracked leather creaking softly beneath me. I can almost see him sitting across from me, his dark hair tousled from running his fingers through it. His blue eyes are intense as he leans in, discussing the intricacies of Shakespeare's sonnets. I can almost hear his voice, deep and rich, like the first sip of fine whiskey.

It burned my throat until he taught me how to drink it.

Memories flood back.

The way his strong hands would gesture as he spoke of Shakespeare. The way his eyes would light up when I challenged him—both academically and sexually. The way he would lean in, his breath hot on my cheek, as he murmured explicit commands.

My heart aches. I press a hand to my chest, as if I can somehow soothe the hurt. But it's not just pain I'm feeling. It's something more. Something darker.

Something that makes my breath hitch.

I close my eyes, and I'm back there.

Back in that moment when his hand brushed mine, sending a jolt of electricity through me. Back in that moment when his gaze dropped to my lips, his eyes darkening with desire. Back in that moment when I realized that he could control me with only a dark gaze.

I remember the feel of his mouth on mine, the taste of him, the heat of him. The way his hands tangled in my hair, the way his body pressed against mine. The way he whispered my name, like a secret, like a sin.

I remember, but I wish I could forget.

I'm flushed, my skin hot and sensitive. I can feel the ghost of his touch, the echo of his kiss. I can feel the ache of desire, the throb of need. My body is confused, caught between the past and the present. Caught between the memory of him and the reality of his absence.

I take a deep, shuddering breath, trying to calm my racing heart. But the scent of the library, the leather under my fingers, the sun streaming through the window…it's too much.

I run my fingers over the worn table, tracing the grooves and imperfections. This was his spot.

Where he'd sit across from me, his eyes darkened with passion as he'd discuss sonnets and soliloquies. I can almost hear his voice, the deep timbre that would send shivers down my spine.

I can almost see his handsome face.

Almost, but not quite.

The chair across from me is empty now.

The table bare, the floor empty.

Except for… I lean in, my brow furrowing.

A black envelope lies on the worn wooden floor, a stark contrast against the dull grain. It's not the kind you'd find in a stationery store. This one is heavy, the paper thick and textured like a whispered secret. The seal is a deep, bloodred—a wax insignia stamped with a familiar crest.

The Shakespeare Society.

I pick it up, my fingers tracing the edges, a shiver running down my spine. The last time I saw an envelope like this, it held an invitation to a world I did not want. A world that killed Professor Stratford.

Part of me wants to burn it, but I know I should see what they've said.

This message must be for me. Who else would come here?

I slide my finger under the seal, breaking it with a soft snap. The paper inside is just as heavy, the ink dark and bold.

> *Beware the ides of inquiry, fair maiden. Cease thy search, lest thou desire to join the Bard in his eternal slumber. His resting place is sacred ground, not meant for prying eyes. Tread not upon his grave, nor seek his remains.*

It's not a long message, but it doesn't need to be.

The words are sharp, cutting, and unmistakably clear.

They want me to stop asking about his burial place.

My breath catches in my throat. It's a threat, thinly veiled in Shakespearean language. They know I've been asking questions, digging into Professor Stratford's death, trying to find out where he's buried. And they don't like it.

I read the note again, my heart pounding in my chest.

It's designed to scare me. And it's working.

It also proves that there's something to uncover.

Where is he buried? Why does the Shakespeare Society care?

I crumple the heavy paper in my fist, hard

edges biting into my palm.

I glance around the empty library, the shelves of books suddenly feeling like eyes watching me. The sun dipping low in the sky, turning the shelves into long shadows. Apprehension is a heavy weight in my stomach, a warning bell ringing in my ears.

I'm alone here. Vulnerable.

Whoever left this note knows that.

I step into the elevator, the metal doors sliding shut with a soft hiss. My reflection stares back at me on the polished surface, eyes wide, cheeks flushed. I take a deep breath, trying to calm my racing heart. The note in my pocket feels like a burning coal.

The elevator lurches to a stop, the doors opening with a ding. I step out, my boots echoing on the marble floor. The library is quiet, the air filled with the scent of old books and dust. I walk quickly, my heart pounding in my chest. I just want to get out of here, to escape the ghosts of the past that seem to haunt every corner of this place. To escape whatever ghost left this note.

I push open the heavy doors, the cool air outside a slap in the face. I take a deep breath, filling my lungs with the scent of fall, crisp leaves and distant smoke. I step forward, my eyes on the ground, my mind a million miles away.

"Hey."

My heart hammers in my chest as I spin around, my eyes wide. Tyler stands there, his hands shoved in his pockets. His brows rise at whatever he sees on my face. "Didn't mean to scare you."

I press a hand to my chest. "You scared the shit out of me."

"Sorry," he says, taking a step back toward the bronze elephant statue. That's why I didn't see him on my way out. He was half hidden. Why? Was he waiting for me? Unlikely. This is a useful library on campus. It's only the strange note making me paranoid.

That doesn't mean I forgive him.

"I'm fine," I say stiffly, shoving the note deeper into my pocket. My heart is still racing, my breath coming in short gasps.

Tyler's eyes search my face. "You're pale as a sheet," he says softly. "You look like you've seen a ghost."

My lips press into a thin line. "I'm... I'm tired," I say, avoiding his gaze.

He clears his throat, his gaze shifting to the side. "About that final exam," he says, his voice hesitant. "Kind of crazy, right?"

I shake my head, a bitter laugh escaping my lips. "Yeah. Crazy."

"What are you gonna write?"

"It doesn't matter what I write," I say, my voice bleak.

Tyler sighs, running a hand through his hair. "Yeah, I guess you're right," he says. "Thorne didn't look like she was gonna give you a fair chance. Then again maybe she'll pass you just to get rid of you."

"Something to look forward to."

Tyler winces, his eyes filled with apology. "I'm sorry for not acknowledging you in class. It was…it was shitty of me."

"It's fine," I say, even though it's not. Even though his dismissal stung like a slap in the face.

"'The silence of a friend is heavier than the blow of an enemy,'" he quotes.

"I don't recognize that."

Tyler gives me a small smile, his eyes filled with sadness. "Pinky and the Brain," he says.

A little amusement rises in me. That's so Tyler. Even so I'm not sure if it absolves him. I'm not sure that it matters. I take a deep breath, my gaze shifting to the side. The sun is setting, the sky a blaze of orange and red. It's beautiful, but all I can see is the darkness creeping in at the edges.

"I have to go," I say, taking a step back.

"Be safe, Anne," he says, his voice barely above a whisper.

CHAPTER SIX

The Devil

IT'S A RELIEF to find Daisy in the room.

She leans over her desk, her nimble fingers manipulating wires and gears, her blonde brows furrowed in concentration. The soft hum of a soldering iron is a soothing background noise, a counterpoint to the silence of the dorm room.

"Hey," I ask, breathless from the brisk wind. And from anticipation. "You know Professor Cormac Stratford, right?"

A little piece of wire snips off, flying onto the carpet. "I guess."

Her reaction strikes me as strange, her blue eyes wide as if she's nervous or something. But I don't have time to decipher it right now. "Do you know where he is?"

"Umm, maybe."

"Can you tell me where?"

"You couldn't get in even if I told you. It's the

engineering lab. Your ID doesn't have access."

"Then come with me."

She finally puts down what she's holding, her expression clearing, as if she's bracing for something. "What do you want with him?"

"I need to know where William is buried. He's his brother. He has to know."

Sympathy floods her blue eyes. "Anne."

"Please."

"You don't need a slab of concrete to tell him how you feel. He's listening wherever you are on earth."

"I don't have faith like you. I don't know if he exists in any other realm. The only thing that ties me to him is his body, but that's not even why I need to find it."

"Then why?"

"Because someone wants me to stop looking."

I show her the warning from the Society.

She reads it, her eyes darkening. When she looks at me, there's nothing soft and glowy about her. Instead she's a fierce warrior. "You can't be seriously thinking of ignoring this. They've already shown what they're capable of. Now you're going to deliberately defy them. Do you have a death wish?"

Since she's the second person to ask me that

today, it makes me wonder if it's true. Maybe some part of me does want to exit, does want to follow William into whatever place he's found himself—whether that's some afterlife or simply the ground. Maybe that's why I'm so obsessed with finding his grave.

"Everyone is so afraid of them," I say, almost bitter. "They hurt us, so we decide to never fight them. What happens when they keep hurting us? Isn't there some point at which we fight back?"

"Fighting back looks like getting enough power to get rid of them. It does not look like sneaking around trying to find a grave that doesn't even matter."

Hurt squeezes my heart. "Fine. Never mind. I'll find him myself."

"Don't be like that."

"I love you, Daisy, but you don't get to control me any more than the Shakespeare Society does. I thought that you, of all people, would understand that."

Her expression softens. She does understand it, because it's what she's been fighting against her whole life. "Anne."

"I shouldn't have involved you. Of course you've been hurt by them. You shouldn't have to help me fight them."

"I'm already involved. I was involved from the moment they dragged me into the van. You already know they drugged me. They thought it made me out of my mind, and it did. I saw some scary shit on whatever pill they forced down my throat. The Devil visited me."

"The Devil?"

"But even as He sat there, pilfering my secrets, stroking my inner wounds, I heard what they were saying."

She's never spoken about this. "You don't have to talk about this."

"I want to. They were taking orders from someone, clearly an adult. I'm assuming now that it was Andini or someone who works for him. One of them wanted to fuck me. Someone our age, but the man said no."

My throat tightens. "God."

"I don't think he was trying to protect me. He knew it would be seen as more than a prank if that happened. It would get more attention in the news. It wasn't part of his plan. He's calculating. Manipulative. And completely insane."

The memory comes to me of the tattered copy of *Macbeth* that's part of the Port Lavaca Library. I returned it, of course, before I left for the summer. Macbeth was also calculating. Manipulative. And completely insane.

How are you supposed to live in a department run by such a man?

He'll never be satisfied with only running the department, of course.

It will be the university as a whole. Maybe even the city.

Does he have enough power for that? Enough ruthlessness?

Maybe.

So I can cower in fear for the rest of the school year. It won't stop him. Won't even slow him down, of course. That's what he wants from me.

I take Daisy's hands in mine and squeeze gently. "Please believe me when I tell you that I know. I know he's really, really, *really* bad. You think that if I'd defy him, then I must not understand that, not fully, but I do. It's a choice to be afraid. And I don't want to live that way."

Her eyes glisten with unshed tears. "I don't want you to get hurt."

"I'm already hurt, and it's only going to get worse. Fear doesn't prevent it. It doesn't protect me." I remember the young girl in the library with the pretend cape and the foam sword, her chin held high, ready to fight the world. A little bean sprout of a girl. It won't keep her safe, not really. I know, because I used to be her. "Being afraid is just…being afraid. That's it. There's no upside."

"You're really wise. You know that?"

That's the lie of trauma and anxiety. It tells us that if we worry enough, if we dedicate our entire lives to stress, that we'll somehow be safer. It's lying. "I'm not wise. I'm well read."

"What's the difference?"

I grin at her. "You know the way to my heart."

"Good," she says. "Because I love you, too. And I'm not going to try to control you. But I am going with you."

"Because I need your ID to get in?"

"No, because he's more likely to tell you what you want to know if I'm with you. I know what he wants."

I don't know much about Cormac Stratford besides the fact that he's William's brother. And a professor of engineering. "Money?"

"No," she says. "Me."

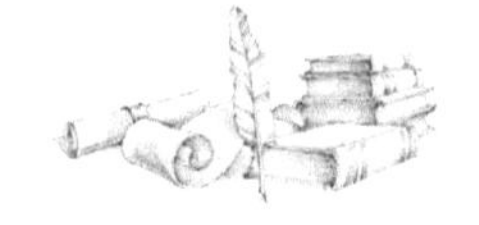

CHAPTER SEVEN
Cruel Dream

IVY COVERS THE old engineering building. It's a relic from a time when engineering consisted on nuts and bolts instead of superconductors and nanobots. The wind whispers secrets through their leaves, sending a shiver down my spine.

The moon hangs low, casting shadows of bare branches.

These ancient oaks have stood here for decades.

They've watched students come and go. They've watched people live and die. Now they're watching us walk alone on a dark street, when we should be back in our dorm room studying. Or at least hanging out in the pub or the student union with friends.

I'm glad Daisy's with me, even though I'm nervous about what she said. What exactly will Cormac require of us to get the information?

Hopefully nothing.

Daisy scans her student ID card, and a light on a black box turns green. I push open the heavy wooden door at her nod. It creaks ominously, echoing through the empty halls. The building is abandoned at this hour. I imagine there are usually students on the benches and at the computers. Now there's only an unsettling silence. Our footsteps echo off the cold stone floors.

Cormac Stratford's office is on the third floor. We climb the staircase, the wooden steps groaning under our weight. The air grows colder, the silence more profound. By the time we reach his office, my heart is pounding in my chest.

Daisy knocks, the sound sharp in the silence.

Then, without waiting, she opens the door, revealing a man with his sleeves rolled up as he leans over some complicated-looking piece of machinery. It's similar to what Daisy looks like in her dorm, only on a much larger scale.

He looks up, his expression stoic even though I sense his surprise.

He gives Daisy a slow, intense once-over, his gaze traveling from her head to her toes. Tension crackles in the room. She wasn't wrong about that. He does want her. His desire is palpable enough to make me feel like an intruder.

Then his gaze shifts to me.

There's a flicker of recognition, but he doesn't acknowledge it. Instead, he raises an eyebrow. "Can I help you?"

"I'm Anne Hill," I say, my voice steady despite the nerves churning in my stomach. "I was a student of Professor Stratford. And…more than a student. I need to know where he's buried."

Cormac's expression darkens. "I can't tell you that."

"Why not?"

"Many reasons."

"I have a right to know."

"Do you?"

"Yes. I loved him."

"Then let his memory rest."

"I can't."

"Professor Stratford," Daisy murmurs. "Please."

It's strange to hear another man called by that name—Professor Stratford. It makes William's memory pulse in the room, almost as if he's here with us. But no, he isn't. She's talking to someone else.

It's also strange to hear the soft, almost submissive voice she used.

As if she's offering what he wants.

There are undercurrents strong enough to drown a person in here. I don't know how they ever manage to actually do engineering.

He shakes his head. "No. It's for her own good."

"My own good?" I echo, frustration burning inside me. "I'm living in hell. I need closure. I need to say goodbye."

His expression doesn't soften. "I can't help you."

I take a deep breath, ready to argue, but Daisy steps forward, placing a hand on my arm. She looks at Cormac, her blue eyes steady. "Please. She needs to do this. We'll do anything. *Anything.*"

Cormac looks at Daisy, his expression unreadable.

The room falls silent, lust like a heartbeat in the room. I hold my breath, waiting for his response, wondering if I should even allow her to make this offer. Probably not, but I also can't bring myself to speak the words to cancel it out.

"Not like this," he says.

I let out a breath, half frustration, half relief.

Daisy turns to me, her blue eyes serious. "Show him."

I hesitate, then pull the crumpled note from

my pocket. The Society's seal is embossed at the top, the paper worn and aged. I hand it to Cormac. He scans it, his brow furrowing.

"You see," she says. "She's in danger. They must be watching her. If you tell her where it is, they won't have any reason to warn her away."

"This wasn't sent by the Society," he says, his voice gruff.

I shake my head. "The seal—"

"And the paper," Daisy adds. "It's the same."

Cormac curses under his breath. "I know who sent it. And since you insist on interrupting my work tonight, I'll take you there. We'll call it getting even."

I exchange a glance with Daisy. "What does that mean?" I whisper.

She shakes her head. "No idea."

He moves around the room, closing up a few mysterious boxes that contain wires, flipping switches, looking like he's packing up to leave. At that point he'll presumably take us to whoever sent the threat.

"Could this be a trap?" I ask. "He could be part of the Society."

She shakes her head. "He hates them. And he can be ruthless, but not about something like this."

It makes me wonder in what way he *can* be ruthless, but then Cormac arrives, shrugging into a coat. He's built with more muscle mass than William. The word beefy comes to mind. William is strong, and even taller, but his musculature is more lean.

"Let's go," Cormac says.

We follow him out of the office, the door clicking shut behind us. The hall is dark, the only light coming from the dim glow of the exit signs. Cormac leads us down a narrow staircase, his footsteps echoing in the silence.

We step outside, the cold air hitting me like a slap.

The night is dark, the moon hidden behind thick clouds.

Cormac leads us through the back alleys of the university, past humming generators and towering air-conditioning units. The path is unfamiliar, the buildings looming above us like silent sentinels.

Even if Cormac isn't leading us into a Society trap, it doesn't feel precisely safe. The university is different at night, the shadows hiding secrets and dangers.

I stay close to Daisy, her presence a comfort in the darkness.

Cormac turns into a metal door, leading us

down a narrow corridor, the walls close and oppressive. The air is thick with dust and dampness.

We reach a door.

He stops suddenly, turning to face us. His eyes are hard, his jaw set. "Listen," he says, his voice low. "What you're about to see… But it's the truth. Maybe you do deserve to know. Either way, it'll be done."

I swallow, my heart pounding in my chest. "I'm ready."

Daisy's hand finds mine, her grip tight.

Cormac nods, then opens the door and disappears into the night. Darkness swallows him, and we hurry to catch up.

We emerge back into the night.

The old cathedral looms before us, its gothic spires clawing at the dusk-streaked sky like skeletal fingers. I remember it, vaguely, passing by on the student tour when I first got here.

It was built when Tanglewood University was still a private college, when it still had religious ties. Eventually it changed hands. Services continued for a while, even though they stopped being mandatory.

Eventually even those stopped.

Has the building been empty all this time?

It must have been.

The air is thick with the scent of decaying leaves and the distant promise of rain. A shiver runs down my spine as I take in the crumbling façade, the once-grand structure now a shadow of its former glory. The stained glass windows, once vibrant and whole, are now dull from decades of dust.

Daisy's hand brushes against mine, a silent reassurance that she's by my side. Her blue eyes scan the cathedral, her expression a mirror of my own unease. "This place gives me the creeps," she whispers.

Me, too. "You don't have to come inside."

"Shut up," she says with affection.

We step inside, the heavy wooden door creaking behind us.

The air is cool and damp, the silence broken only by the distant drip of water and the echo of our footsteps. The cathedral is a labyrinth of shadows, the faded grandeur of its vaulted ceilings and ornate columns marred by the passage of time and the encroachment of nature.

Cormac stands in front of us, not looking particularly concerned about the dismal state of the building. "Get out here."

Is he talking to us?

No, he's talking to someone else, someone inside the building.

Someone who sent me a letter.

Someone who knows more than they should about me.

A figure emerges from the darkness, his silhouette stark against the dim light filtering through the broken windows. William Stratford, his handsome features more rugged, his eyes burning with blue fire. He's a commanding presence, his broad shoulders and muscular frame a testament to his strength.

A wave of dizziness washes over me, the world tilting on its axis.

I reach out, my hand grasping the cold stone wall for support. Daisy catches me. This can't be true. I held him as he took his last breath. His death was reported in the news. I felt his loss like a physical wound.

"Hello, Anne."

"Oh God." Daisy's voice.

I hear Cormac explaining, but he sounds tinny, as if I'm hearing him over a poor phone connection. "William needed to make the Society believe he was dead. It was either that or let them kill him."

The options were to die…or to die.

A laugh bubbles up from deep within me, a sound of pure, unadulterated joy. I clap a hand over my mouth, trying to stifle the sound, but it's no use. The laughter spills out, echoing through the cathedral, a stark contrast to the somber atmosphere. I sound hysterical. I *am* hysterical.

He takes a step closer—beautiful and strong and *breathing*.

More gaunt, I realize. With a shadow on his jaw. He was always shaved close before. He's different, but he's still alive.

"It's okay, brave heart. I'm here now."

A sob tears from my throat, raw and primal, clawing its way out from the depths of my soul. I press my fists against my chest, as if the physical pain can somehow dull the emotional turmoil raging within me.

"You," I gasp, the word a choked whisper. "You, you, you."

He comes close enough to touch. The same piercing eyes, the same chiseled jaw, the same commanding presence that had once captivated me. There's a new tension in his stance, a wariness in his gaze that speaks of what he's endured, what his fake death has cost him.

"Yes," he says, his voice a low rumble. "Me."

A dam breaks within me, a flood of emotions

surging forth. Relief, joy, anger, sorrow—they all crash over me, wave after wave, threatening to pull me under. My fists beat against my chest, a futile attempt to contain the storm raging within me. Tears stream down my cheeks, hot and bitter, a testament to the grief I had carried, the loss I had mourned.

A sob escapes, the sound echoing through the cathedral, a haunting melody of heartache and release. I look up at him, my eyes swimming with tears, my breath hitching in my chest. And then I'm falling, dissolving into him, my body pressed against his. His arms wrap around me, a fortress of strength, a sanctuary I thought I'd lost.

My sobs come harder now, wracking my body, purging the grief and the pain, the fear and the sorrow. I cling to him, my fingers digging into his back, my face pressed against his chest. His heart beats steadily beneath my ear, a soothing rhythm that anchors me, grounds me in the here and now.

"I'm here," he whispers, his breath warm against my hair.

I cry harder, the tears flowing freely, a river of release.

It's cathartic, this letting go, this purging of the emotions I had kept bottled up for so long. I had mourned him, had grieved for him, had believed him lost to me forever. But he's here now, alive and real and solid in my arms.

The bastard.

His hands stroke my back, a soothing touch that seems to calm the storm within me. His lips press against my forehead, a soft, gentle kiss that speaks of comfort and care.

I melt into him, my body molding to his, my breath syncing with his.

The world seems to fade away, the shadows of the cathedral retreating, the weight of my grief lifting. There's only him and me, only this moment, only this connection that transcends time and space, that defies logic and reason.

It defies death.

I pull back slightly, my eyes meeting his. His gaze is intense, a swirling mix of emotions that mirror my own. There's so much to say, so much to ask, so much to understand, so much to be afraid of.

For now, there's only us.

Only him.

Only the impossible.

I'm not sure how long I cry. Long enough that I'm hollowed out inside. He holds me. When I pull back, I see familiar, beloved, handsome features bathed in the ethereal light, and a part of me wonders if this is real.

Maybe he isn't alive.

Maybe this is just a cruel dream, a figment of my grief-stricken imagination. But the heat of his touch anchors me in the here and now.

CHAPTER EIGHT

Crossword Puzzle

S OMEHOW CORMAC AND Daisy fall away. It occurs to me that I should check on her. That I should confirm that she won't have to pay any kind of price for helping me tonight. The way he looked at her—it wasn't safe.

It reminds me of the way William looks at me.

Or the way he used to.

Now his expression is more opaque, his eyes dark.

He's harder to read.

That pisses me off. He should be an open book by now. When you've torn yourself apart over a man, he shouldn't get to be a mystery.

He leads me up the stairs, and I'm too bone-less to argue the point. Or to wonder where we're going. It's the bell tower. There's still a thick metal bar across the top with a welded-on circle for a chain. No bell, though. I wonder when they decided to remove it. And how it even got out of here without them demolishing the tower.

The open space in the floor where it would have rung has been boarded over long ago, from the state of it. There's a bed in the corner, on the floor, the sheets mussed. I wonder if that's where he was when we showed up. I wonder if he saw us coming from the stained glass windows. They paint him in a blue light that removes any hint of remorse, if he even had any to begin with.

The air is thick with dust and the scent of old stone, the silence broken only by the distant hum of the campus below. The heavy glass windows filter in an eerie blue light, casting everything in a dreamlike glow. It's as if we're underwater, trapped in a forgotten world where time has no meaning.

"Ahhh, softly now," William murmurs, his voice closer now. I can feel the heat of his body, the solid strength of his presence. "You're all right."

"All right? I'm not all right. You let me believe you were dead."

"I know."

"You let me mourn you," I say, my voice broken.

"Yes."

"How could you?" I whisper, my voice echoing in the hollow space.

"The Society needed to believe I was gone. It was the only way to keep you safe, to keep us both safe. It had to be real."

I wipe away hot, angry tears. "So this was planned?"

"Not at first. I thought I was being careful. Not careful enough, apparently. I got a call from Brandon's mother. She sounded distraught. She told me that Brandon was in trouble. I ran into a trap."

"And…what? You worked with the Shakespeare Society to fake your death?"

His eyes darken. "How could you ask me that?"

I pull out the black envelope, now crumpled from my anxiety and the journey. We made it into hell, me and this piece of vellum. "You sent this, right? You're the one who threatened me."

"It wasn't a threat. It was a warning."

"Oh good. That's less ominous."

"If you kept looking into my death, wanting to know the location of the grave, then they would have guessed it was a ruse. And moreover, it would have made you a target. They already proved they were capable of murder."

"You know what would have made me not look for your grave?"

"Anne."

"If I didn't think you were *dead.*"

"I wasn't working with the Shakespeare Society. Don't think that for a second. I was working against them, fighting them, but I was getting too close. And they were getting too powerful. I couldn't risk you."

A bitter laugh escapes me. "Yes, it would be terrible if I knew a secret. I meet so many Shakespearean scholars in Port Lavaca. I would surely have been unable to hold it inside. It's so much better that I cried for months."

Sympathy flashes across his eyes.

I can't stand sympathy.

"Did Brandon know?"

He pauses. A fatal pause.

"He did. So your brother knew. Brandon knew. Did the *New York Times* know? Maybe it was in their crossword puzzle. *The Shakespearean professor who may or may not be dead.* Everyone knew except me."

"It was only them."

"Oh, only them."

"They're family."

That hurts worse than sympathy.

I'm not his family. I knew that.

So it shouldn't feel like I've been poisoned, like I'm lying on the ground, needing a paramedic. The fight leaves me. The righteous indignation? Gone.

There's only the desolate acknowledgment that yes, of course.

I wasn't important enough to tell.

"Great," I say, turning toward the stairs.

He pulls me back. "It wasn't like that."

"Then what was it like? Did you sit around laughing about it, the clueless kid who thought she mattered? I'm sure it was great entertainment. *The Taming of the Student.*"

"Stop."

"No, you're right. It wasn't funny. It was more like an experiment. It would make a great paper. *Tragic Romance in Modern-Day Women.* What happens if she thinks her lover dies? Does she or does she not kill herself?"

His eyes flash. "*Stop.*"

There are too many feelings inside me to stop. Anger and fear and grief. Leftover grief, so much of it that I'm not sure it will ever leave, even now that he's alive. There's nothing left to grieve, except my trust.

"I hate you."

"Good," William says, his voice a low growl.

"I hate you so much."

"You should hate me. I've cursed your name every night that I've spent alone in this tower. You should hate me the way I hate you. Hate me so hard it feels like love."

"Never."

Anger surges within me, a hot, pulsating force that demands release. I step forward, my hands reaching for his collar, my fingers gripping the fabric tightly.

He doesn't resist, doesn't pull away.

Instead, he leans into me, his hands cupping my face, his thumbs brushing away the tears that stream down my cheeks.

"I would do it again," he murmurs.

That breaks my heart.

It's what he'll always do—break my heart.

I kiss him then, angrily, fiercely. My lips crush against his, my teeth nipping at his lower lip. It's a kiss born of fury and frustration, a kiss that demands retribution, that seeks to punish.

And he lets me.

He takes it, absorbs it, his hands soothing me, his touch gentle even as my kiss is not. "It's okay," he whispers against my lips. "I'm here. Don't cry, brave heart."

Tears stream down my face, mixing with our kiss, the saltiness a stark contrast to the sweetness of his lips.

His hands move to my hair, his fingers tangling in the strands. He deepens the kiss, his tongue sliding against mine, a slow, sensuous dance that sends shivers down my spine. I can taste his desperation, his hunger, his need. It mirrors my own, a frantic, clawing desire that demands to be sated.

I push him back, my hands fumbling with his shirt, my fingers trembling as I unbutton it. He helps me, his hands steady, his gaze never leaving mine. His shirt falls to the floor, a puddle of white against the dusty stone. His chest is bare, the muscles taut and defined, the skin smooth and warm.

His hands reach for my shirt, his fingers mirroring my earlier actions. He undresses me slowly, reverently, his eyes drinking in every inch of exposed skin. I stand before him, bare and vulnerable, the cool air a stark contrast to the heat of his gaze.

"Touch me," he says, his voice a low growl that sends shivers down my spine. "Feel me. Punish me if you have to, anything but leave."

I reach out, my fingers tentative, brushing against his chest. His skin is warm, the muscle beneath firm. His heart beats steadily under my palm, a rhythm that grounds me, anchors me in the present.

He's alive. He's truly alive.

A sob catches in my throat, a mix of relief and lingering disbelief. I press my palm flat against his chest, feeling the thrum of his heartbeat, letting it resonate through me. His hands cover mine, his fingers intertwining with my own, squeezing gently.

"I'm here," he murmurs, his eyes never leaving mine. "I'm right here."

I nod, swallowing hard, trying to push down the lump in my throat. I need to feel him, to reconnect with him, to reassure myself that this is real. My hand slides down his chest. I form a claw, scratching my way down, leaving red marks. I'm not gentle. I want it to hurt.

The clock hands above us cast heavy shadows, frozen in place, a stark reminder that for us, time has stopped.

William's hands are on me, urgent and insistent. He traces the curves of my body, his touch leaving trails of fire in its wake, gentle where I'm sharp. I gasp as he lifts me, setting me down on the dusty table that sits beneath the frozen clock. The wood is cool against my bare skin, a sharp contrast to the heat of his touch.

He kneels before me, his eyes never leaving mine. His hands slide up my thighs, pushing them apart, opening me up to him. I'm exposed, vulnerable, but with William, I feel safe. I feel wanted.

"So beautiful," he says, his voice a low rumble that vibrates through me. His fingers trace the edges of my folds, teasing, tantalizing. I squirm, trying to press myself closer to his touch, but he holds me firm, his grip strong and sure.

He leans in, his breath hot against my core. I shiver in anticipation, my fingers tangling in his hair, urging him closer. He doesn't make me wait long. His tongue delves into me, a slow, sensuous exploration that has me gasping for breath. He licks and suckles, his tongue tracing intricate patterns that leave me writhing and moaning.

Pressure builds, a coil tightening deep within me, an otherworldly pleasure. His tongue is relentless, his mouth devouring me, pushing me closer and closer to the edge.

"Professor," I gasp, my voice echoing in the hollow space. His name is a plea, a prayer, a desperate cry for release. He answers, his fingers sliding into me, his mouth suckling my clit, his teeth grazing the sensitive bud.

I shatter, my body convulsing as waves of pleasure crash over me. I cry out, my voice echoing through the bell tower, a symphony of ecstasy and relief. The world spins, the blue light swirling around me, the shadows dancing and shifting.

As the waves subside, I collapse back onto the table, my body limp, my breath coming in ragged gasps. William stands, his eyes dark with desire, his lips glistening with my release. I reach for him, my fingers tracing the lines of his face, the stubble on his jaw.

"Daisy," I murmur, suddenly remembering that we're not alone in this place. William chuckles, a low, wry sound that sends shivers down my spine.

"They won't bother us," he says, his voice a husky growl. "Cormac will take care of her, make sure she gets back to her dorm room."

"Did you know he was going to bring me here?"

"No, and he shouldn't have taken the risk. But I can't regret that it happened. Not if I get to hold you tonight."

"Aren't you worried I'm going to tell someone?"

A low growl. "I always trusted you."

"Daisy knows, too. Are you going to silence her? Is Cormac?"

"No, damn it."

"You went through a lot of trouble for secrecy."

"Yes, because my plan only works like this."

"What *is* your plan?"

His silence pulses in the blue-black room. It's a bruise, this tower. A physical manifestation of pain. "It's better if you don't know."

"Right," I say, my voice hollow. "You still don't trust me."

"It's about risk. The fewer people who know, the better."

"You're allowed to endanger yourself, but I'm supposed to sit in ignorance. As if that even makes me safe, when I have to go to class every day with Professor Thorne."

He tenses. "Steer clear of her."

"Oh, sure. That'll be easy to do."

"I'm serious. Go to class. Keep your head down. Don't talk to her any more than you have to."

"Too late."

"What the hell does that mean?"

I tell him about the fake manuscript, my idea for exposing her as a fraud, my little retribution for his death. Now that I found out he's alive, I'm not exactly going to take it back. She deserves it, anyway.

He's quiet for a moment. I'm waiting for him to chastise me.

When I look over, he's fighting a smile. "Damn, brave heart."

"I thought you'd be mad."

"Of course I am. I don't want you in harm's way."

"Too bad. We live in this world, the dangerous one."

He swears, a mixture of modern terms and old Shakespearean curses. "You can't tell anyone you saw me, Anne. You know that, but I'm making it explicit. You have to act natural. However you were yesterday and the day before, that's how you have to look."

"Fine."

"And you can't attract their attention. Not for any reason."

He's being autocratic. I shouldn't find it hot. "Yes, Professor."

"Call me William, for God's sake."

"Then stop looking at me with that stern

professor face."

"Call me William when I'm fucking you." He leans down, capturing my lips in a fierce kiss. I can taste myself on him, a heady, intoxicating mix that sends a fresh wave of desire coursing through me. His hands roam my body, rekindling the fire that burns within me.

There's more to ask. More to wonder about.

It can wait.

He enters me in one swift thrust, filling me completely. I gasp, my body arching to meet his. He begins to move, his hips pistoning against mine, his cock sliding in and out of me in a rhythm that leaves me breathless.

"I came back so I could fuck this pretty little cunt." His voice is a low growl, the filthy words spilling from his lips like a secret, a promise, like Shakespeare. They are without artifice. They sound like truth. "Came back from the dead so I could fuck you one more time."

I shudder, the words wrapping around me, the rhythm of his body pushing me higher and higher. The coil tightens again, the pressure building, the world spinning.

Blue light swirls around us, a midnight ocean.

"William," I gasp, my body tightening as another orgasm crashes over me. He groans, his body shuddering, his cock pulsing within me as he finds his own release. I watch his face, the lines etched with desire, the muscles taut, the eyes dark and intense. He's handsome, vital, alive. But beneath it all, there's a shadow, a lingering danger that refuses to fade.

His body collapses onto mine, his breath coming in ragged gasps, his heart pounding against my chest. I wrap my arms around him, holding him close, refusing to let go. We lie there, our bodies entwined, our breaths mingling, our hearts beating.

Beating, because we're alive.

Despite the blue tint of our skin, alive.

CHAPTER NINE

The Stronger Student

MY HEART HAMMERS in my chest as I walk into the lecture hall.

I'm supposed to act normal, though I'm not even sure what that would be. Angry? Sad? I definitely shouldn't look as if I made love to William Stratford only hours ago.

I keep my head down, avoiding eye contact as I make my way to my usual seat in the back. I'm exhausted, my body still humming from last night. My skin tingles with the memory of his touch, his kiss, his body moving against mine. I can still feel him, still taste him, still hear his voice whispering filthy words.

I squeeze my eyes shut, pushing the pleasure away.

I can't think about that now.

Not here, not with Thorne watching.

Professor Thorne speaks as she begins class. I

can't focus. I'm too aware of my own body, of the way my clothes rub against my skin, of the way my heartbeat echoes in my ears. I shift in my seat, uncomfortable, my body aching in places that make my cheeks flush.

Thorne's looking at me, her expression inscrutable.

Does she know? Can she tell? Of course not.

But I look away, my heart pounding even harder.

I force myself to scratch out words with my pencil, mindlessly taking notes as she delivers her lecture. I write about deception, about betrayal, about the destructive power of unchecked ambition.

She pulls out a stack of papers. "Your assignments," she says.

The entire room sits up a little straighter.

I already know what's coming. She will dismiss most of the class as being beneath her notice. She'll praise her protégé, Matteo, who so conveniently happens to be the son of Andini. At least he doesn't seem to be preening. Instead he seems almost sad.

Then, she'll probably rip mine apart.

"I tasked you with exploring the theme of reality versus illusion in *Macbeth*. Some of you"—

she pauses, her gaze landing on a few unlucky souls—"failed to grasp even the basic concept."

She drops a few papers onto the podium.

"Others showed a modicum of understanding, but lacked the insight to truly delve into the theme."

More pages join the discard pile.

"However," she says, her voice dropping to a dramatic whisper, "there was one student who not only understood the theme but explored it with such depth, such insight, that it was a brilliant piece of literary analysis."

Instead of looking at Matteo, she glances at me.

"The witches are often dismissed as plot devices, inciting incidents for Macbeth's ambitions. This student argued that they are not the cause but the effect, that they are illusions created by grandiosity. They allow him to justify his actions, actions he would have taken anyway. It's a compelling argument."

What the hell?

Why would Thorne praise me?

The idea that I wrote something interesting doesn't qualify as a reason. Not for someone like her. I force myself to mouth the words "thank you."

Let her believe that I'm grateful for her approval.

She nods and continues her lecture, her voice echoing through the hall as she dissects the second act of *Macbeth*. What is she planning? The class ticks by, each minute stretching into an eternity. I'm hyperaware of every sound, every movement, every breath. The scratch of pens on paper, the rustle of notebooks, the hum of the fluorescent lights—it's all amplified, overwhelming.

Finally, the class draws to a close.

Thorne wraps up her lecture, her voice fading away as the students around me begin to pack up their things.

As I stand up, her voice cuts through the noise.

"Ms. Hill," she says, her tone pleasant, almost friendly. She smiles, a warm smile that doesn't quite reach her eyes. "A moment, please."

I freeze, my heart leaping into my throat.

"Of course, Professor," I manage to say, my voice steady despite the turmoil inside me. I make my way down to the podium, my steps slow, measured. Instead of speaking to me there, she has me follow her into the office.

This is Professor Stratford's office.

Except it's not, of course.

He doesn't have one, considering he's supposedly dead.

It's her office now. She's made changes. It's painted something darker. Gone are the many tomes that probably came with the room. Now the shelves are filled with award plaques, framed certificates, and photographs of Thorne herself standing in front of notable places. I recognize the thatched roof of the house where Shakespeare was born, the funerary monument erected after his death.

One photo shows her standing on the stage of the Globe Theatre, surrounded by the cast of *Macbeth*, still in character. That one hurts. It's my dream to visit there, even though that will most likely never happen. And if it did, I would be a tourist, someone with a regular ticket, not a VIP like she clearly is.

"You have a real talent for analysis," she says. "I'm impressed."

"Thank you," I say, because we're both playing parts as surely as if we walked the boards of the Globe. I just have to wait for what she wants.

"I also wanted to talk to you about something else," she continues, her voice dropping to a conspiratorial whisper. "The book you had the other day. I know why you tried to hide it from me."

My heart stops. She does?

"You are a smart girl, so you understood how important it is. So you wanted to keep it for yourself."

I try not to show my relief.

"I think you and I could work together," she says, her voice soft, persuasive. "I think we could collaborate, explore the themes in that book, delve into the mysteries it contains. And when we publish, your name could go on the piece."

Not likely. I don't want my name anywhere near it. Not that she has any intention of following through with such a promise. "I don't know."

"Of course," she says, her understanding voice belied by the predatory gleam in her eyes. "You are concerned about loyalty, but Stratford wouldn't want you to squander this. Opportunities like this don't come along every day."

I grip the strap of my bag tighter, my knuckles turning white. I want to shove her offer in her face, want to tell her that I'd rather eat glass than work with her. She's probably only asking me this because she needs to know more about the provenance of the book, but I can use that. If I get closer to her, if I learn her secrets, maybe I can find a way to bring her down.

It seems unlikely, but it also feels like it's worth a chance.

"I...I don't know," I stammer, letting my nerves show. I look down, my eyes fixed on the worn wooden floor of the lecture hall. "I mean, Professor Stratford told me I'm supposed to keep it a secret."

Thorne's nostrils flare in excitement. Her voice comes out soft, like she's coaxing a small animal from its burrow. "Precisely. It must be handled very carefully. He understood that. That's why we won't tell anyone that we're working on this. If they ask, we'll simply tell them that I'm giving you tutoring. There are so few prominent women in the field, I had to help."

I take a deep breath, my heart pounding in my chest. I can do this. I can play her game. I look up, my eyes meeting hers. "I think maybe that's why it hurt so much when you picked Matteo to work with."

She leans in, her voice dropping to a conspiratorial whisper. "The only reason I did that is because of my connection with Andini. You are the stronger student, the more promising scholar. I see a spark that reminds me of myself when I was your age. I want to nurture that, to help you succeed."

I swallow hard, my mind racing. She's playing right into my hands. I let my shoulders relax, let my breath come a little easier. I look up at her, my eyes wide, eager. "You're right, Professor Thorne. I can't...I can't pass up this opportunity. I want to learn from you. I want to work with you."

Thorne's smile returns, her eyes gleaming with triumph. "Excellent," she says, her voice brisk, businesslike. "We'll start right away. I want you to come to my office tomorrow afternoon. Bring all of your notes that you took regarding the book, anything that relates to its origins, to where he found it. I also want to know if he's discussed the book with anyone else."

Of course she wants to know that, considering she plans to steal his work. I nod, trying to look eager. "I won't let you down."

She smiles, her eyes gleaming. "I know you won't."

As I walk out of the office, my heart pounding, my mind racing, I can't shake the feeling that I've made a deal with the devil. It's too late to turn back now. I have to hope that I can come out on top, that I can take Thorne down before she takes me down with her.

CHAPTER TEN

Dangerous Games

'M BARELY THROUGH the door of the bell tower before William's hands are on me, his mouth hot and desperate on mine.

I moan under the assault, my body pressing against his, my need for him overwhelming. His tongue slides against mine, his hands roaming my body, gripping, squeezing, possessing.

"Fuck," he growls, his voice low, urgent. His hands are at the hem of my shirt, pulling it up, over my head. I gasp as his mouth finds my neck, his teeth grazing my skin, his stubble rough against my softness.

My hands are at his shirt, fumbling with the buttons. I need to feel him, need to touch him. He helps me, his fingers quick and sure, and then his shirt is off, his chest bare, his muscles taut and defined. I run my hands over him, my fingers tracing the lines of his body, the scars that mark his skin.

"Did anyone follow you?" he asks, his voice harsh, his eyes intense.

I shake my head, my breath coming in gasps. "I was careful."

He nods, his jaw tight. "I hate letting you go out there, unprotected."

"I never want to leave this tower."

His eyes darken. "Maybe I won't let you. Maybe I'll tie you to my bed and use you and fuck you. And most of all, hold you."

Before I can manage a reply, his mouth finds mine again, his kiss hungry, fierce. His hands are at my jeans, unbuttoning, unzipping, pushing them down. I kick them off, my body trembling with need, with anticipation.

He lifts me, his hands gripping my ass, my legs wrapping around his waist. He carries me to the table, the one where he used to sit, where he used to watch me. He sets me down, his hands running up my thighs, his thumbs brushing against my core. I gasp, my hips bucking, my body desperate for more.

He leans down, his mouth finding my breast, his tongue circling my nipple, his teeth grazing, biting. I cry out, my hands in his hair, my body arching against him. He moves to the other breast, his hands never leaving my body, never stopping their exploration, their possession.

William pulls out dark red ropes from a worn, wooden chest. They're soft to the touch, yet strong, a deep wine color that's only slightly faded with time. My eyes widen as he leans forward, his intent clear.

"What are those for?" I ask, a tremor in my voice.

In answer, he leans down, his mouth capturing mine in a searing kiss. Before I know it, he's wrapping them around my wrists. I struggle, a mix of concern and arousal coursing through me.

"William…" I start to say.

He smiles—a dangerous smile that makes my heart race.

"These are the bell ropes," he says, his voice low as he secures the other end of the rope to wooden posts built into the tower.

I test the ropes, tugging at them. They're heavy, the knot firm, the fibers velvety against my skin. "Why are they so thick?" I ask, my breath hitching as he trails a finger down my chest, circling my nipple.

"They're strong, made to hold the weight of the bell, but also surprisingly soft," he says, his voice husky. "Over a thousand pounds."

"That's—" I gasp as his hand pinches my nipple. "A lot."

"Yes, but it wasn't a clumsy instrument. It could play mathematical patterns with precision, especially under the right hands." He leans down, his mouth hot on my breast, his tongue circling my nipple, mirroring his words.

I gasp, arching into his touch, my body already on fire.

He moves to the other breast, lavishing it with the same attention. I squirm, the ropes creaking as I pull at them, but there's no give. I'm at his mercy, unable to escape the pleasure he's inflicting on me.

"This is blasphemous," I breathe, my body trembling as he trails kisses down my stomach.

He looks up at me, his eyes dark and dangerous in the dim light of the tower. "Is it?" he asks, his voice a low rumble. He dips his head between my thighs, his breath hot on my pussy.

I blink, my mind working sluggishly through the pleasure. "It must have been gone for a long time."

He pauses, his breath still hot on me. "Yes."

"Then how did you…"

He looks up at me, his eyes meeting mine. "Taking care of the ropes and the bell was part of my duties," he says. "I was an altar boy."

Oh God. An altar boy.

I'm tied up with rope in a cathedral.

Blasphemous doesn't even cover it.

Before I can process it, he dips his head, his mouth hot on my clit, sucking, licking, driving me wild. I cry out, my body arching, my hands gripping the ropes as pleasure courses through me.

William's mouth is relentless, his tongue circling my clit with a precision that has me seeing stars. He nips, teases, bites, and licks, driving me to the edge of madness. I can feel his fingers, first one, then two, pumping inside me, curling, reaching a spot that has me gasping, my body convulsing with pleasure.

"Please," I cry out, my voice echoing in the tower, bouncing off the cold stone walls. The sound is eerie, haunting, a symphony of my desperation. It's the sound of the bell, the one that's no longer here, its echo lingering, a ghost of its past.

William growls against me, the vibration of his voice sending shivers down my spine. "You taste so fucking good." His tongue licks long and deep. "I could feast on you for hours."

I squirm, the ropes creaking, the wooden table beneath me groaning. I'm at his mercy, unable to escape the pleasure he's inflicting on me. My body is on fire, my skin slick with sweat, my breath coming in short, sharp gasps.

He sucks my clit into his mouth, his fingers pumping faster, harder. Harder. Faster. Tighter. Pleasure coils tight in my belly. I'm close, so close.

"Please," I cry out again, my voice a desperate whimper. "Please, William."

He hums against me, the sound low, approving. "That's it, brave heart. Beg for me."

I do. I beg, my words incoherent, my pleas desperate. I'm not above begging, not when it comes to him. Not when it comes to this.

His tongue flicks against me, his fingers curling, reaching, driving me higher, pushing me closer. I can feel it, the edge, the precipice. I'm right there, teetering, ready to fall.

"Come for me, Anne," he growls, his voice a command, a demand. "Let me hear you scream."

And I do. I scream, my body convulsing, my orgasm crashing over me like a wave. It's intense, overwhelming, a pleasure so profound it's almost painful. I ride it out, my body shaking, my breath coming in sobs.

But William doesn't stop. He doesn't give me time to recover. His mouth is on me again, his tongue lapping at me, his fingers pumping, driving me higher, pushing me further.

"I can't," I gasp, my body trembling. "It's too much."

He chuckles, the sound dark, dangerous. "It's never enough," he says. "Not with you. Not with us."

And he's right. It's not enough. I want more. I need more. I need him.

His mouth is relentless, his tongue circling, flicking, driving me mad. The pressure builds again, the pleasure coiling tight. I'm close, so close.

I'm right there, teetering on the edge, ready to fall. And then, suddenly, William stops. He pulls away, his mouth glistening, his eyes dark, intense.

I whimper, my body trembling, my breath coming in gasps. "Why did you stop?" I ask, my voice a desperate plea.

He smiles, that dangerous smile that makes my heart race. "Because," he says, his voice a low rumble. "I want to hear you beg for it again."

That's what he does.

He drives me mad with lust.

My pleading cries bounce off the walls. They become the sound of the bell. They echo and echo, mathematical patterns with precision, under his skillful hands.

"William," I moan, my voice desperate, pleading. "Please, I need you."

He looks up at me, his eyes dark, hungry. He stands, his hands going to his belt, unbuckling, unzipping. He pushes his jeans down, his cock springing free, hard, ready. I reach for him, wanting to touch, but I'm tied up.

He groans, watching me squirm in the ropes, enjoying it. "That's right," he growls, his voice low, warning. "Remind me I'm alive."

I spread my legs open. "Remind yourself."

He growls, his body covering mine, his cock pressing against my entrance. He pauses, his eyes meeting mine, his expression intense, serious. "I dreamed about this."

I shiver, as if he really did come back from the dead, my body trembling, my need for him overwhelming. It shouldn't be hot. The flames lick my skin. "About what?"

"About this cunt," he says, his voice low, possessive. "And that mouth. Even your ass. Because I'm never letting you go. You're mine. Now and forever."

And then he's inside me, his cock filling me, stretching me, possessing me. I cry out, my body arching against his, my hands gripping his shoulders, his back, his ass. He moves inside me, his thrusts slow, deep, deliberate. I meet each one, my body moving with his, my hips rising, falling, my breath coming in gasps, in moans, in cries.

The bell tower is filled with the sound of us, the sound of our bodies coming together, the sound of our pleasure, our need, our love. The blue light filters in, casting shadows, creating a dreamlike atmosphere.

I struggle to catch my breath, my body slick with sweat, my heart pounding in my chest. William's body is heavy on mine, his breath hot on my neck, his cock still inside me, pulsing with the aftershocks of his release.

I tug at my wrists, the ropes chafing against my skin. "William," I say, my voice a soft plea. "Release me."

He lifts his head, his eyes meeting mine. There's a darkness in them, a possessiveness that sends a shiver down my spine. "Maybe I won't," he says, his voice a low growl.

Panic rises in my chest, a fluttering sensation that makes my breath hitch. I force it down, my voice steady as I say, "Of course you have to. I can't stay here forever."

His hand trails down my body, his fingers brushing against my pussy. I squirm, but this time it's not in pleasure. I'm sore, my body aching from his touch, his cock. "William," I say, my voice a whisper. "I can't. I'm sore."

He leans down, his mouth hot on my ear. "I can make you like it," he murmurs, his voice a dark promise.

I tug harder at the ropes, my voice firm. "You have to let me go."

He lifts his head, his eyes meeting mine. There's a look in them, a look of such imperious desire that it makes my heart race, my body tremble. For a moment, I wonder if he really will keep me here, tied up, at his mercy.

I soften my voice, my body relaxing beneath his. "If I don't show up at class, Thorne will get suspicious."

Only then does a cool resignation enter his eyes. Then, with a sigh, he reaches up, his fingers deftly untying the ropes. I rub my wrists, the skin burning, even though they're barely red or chafed. It's the memory that hurts.

As soon as I'm free, I curl into him, my body seeking his warmth, his comfort. I'm unnerved by his behavior, by the darkness in his eyes, the possessiveness in his touch. But I still want him, need him.

Or need safety.

They're starting to feel like the same thing.

He wraps his arms around me, his body a solid, comforting presence. I can hear his heartbeat, steady, strong. I close my eyes, my body relaxing, my breath evening out.

Even as I lie in his arms, I can't shake off the feeling of unease, the question that lingers in the back of my mind. What if he hadn't let me go?

No, that's crazy. Of course he did.

It was only a game.

The same way the Shakespeare Society plays dangerous games?

I trace patterns on William's chest, our bodies still entwined, our breaths slowly returning to normal. The blue light of the windows casts long shadows, creating an intimate dream where it's just the two of us.

Reality lingers at the edges, waiting to intrude.

"Thorne asked me to stay after class today," I say, my voice soft, hesitant. William's arm tightens around me, his body tensing.

"What did she want?" he asks, his voice a low rumble.

"She wanted to talk about the fake manuscript. Wanted me to work on it with her. Dangled credit on the paper."

"She's lying."

"Well, that'll be handy, since I don't want my

name associated with it. I suspect part of the reason she wants me is because she has to learn where you supposedly got it."

"You told her to go to hell."

I don't say anything.

"Right?" he asks with a growl.

I sit up, the sheet pooling around my waist, my eyes meeting his. "If I can gain her trust, if I can get close to her, maybe I can find something we can use against her. Something that will expose her for what she really is."

William reaches up, his hand cupping my cheek, his thumb brushing against my skin. "I don't want you putting yourself in danger. Thorne is ruthless. She won't hesitate to use you, to hurt you if it suits her purposes."

I cover his hand with mine, my eyes never leaving his. "I can't sit back and do nothing. Not when I have the chance to make a difference. Not when I have the chance to help you."

"I don't need your help. I have a plan."

"One you can't tell me about."

"You have to trust me."

"I'll be careful," I say. "I promise."

He swears, a mixture of modern terms and old Shakespearean curses.

Hurt flickers in my chest. "Don't you trust

me?"

"It's not about trust. It's about safety. Someone found out about us before. Which means someone can find out again."

I stiffen, pulling away from him. "We were having sex in the library, for God's sake. It was a wonder it wasn't discovered sooner."

Frustration bubbles inside me. "Who would I even tell?"

"That's my question to you."

"What does that mean?"

"It means someone found out about our affair."

He's talking about Tanglewood Tea, from before. "They have a million sources. They're always figuring out gossip. Maybe they even tap into the security cameras."

"And one of them knew. So who did you tell?"

"No one. No one who would share it, at least. Daisy knew, but she had more reason to hate the Shakespeare Society than me."

"No one else?"

"Of course not, I—" I pause, remembering the conversation I had with Carlisle where I told her I was having romance troubles. Maybe I hinted that it was a forbidden relationship. I didn't say he was a professor, though.

Narrowed eyes study me. "Who are you thinking of?"

No, that wasn't nearly enough to actually guess what was happening. And as Carlisle mentioned, Tanglewood Tea didn't actually say my name. Why would they leave that piece out if she was the source?

Then again, she seemed pretty sure about what the post included. It had come up in conversation in the middle of campus. She didn't even have to pull up the old post to check what it said.

Still. There's no way.

Tanglewood Tea has slammed her as hard as anyone, mocking the pop princess for her groupies, for the paparazzi on campus, for being stuck up. Why would she help them by giving information about a friend?

Except that…maybe it was a trade.

They couldn't give her money or fame. She already has that. They could lay off her, though. Would she trade me in for a break?

Chills race over my skin. "No one."

"Anne."

"It's *no one*."

He studies me, his eyes narrowed.

I'm not a great liar, but the thing is, I'm not lying.

I have no proof that Carlisle did anything, so I refuse to even utter her name under suspicion. She's shown me nothing but loyalty.

For a pop princess to befriend little Anne Hill?

It's ridiculous.

It's always been ridiculous.

Oh, I know the appeal I have to her. Someone who's far too bookish to even keep up with celebrity gossip. Someone who isn't angling for a selfie for social clout, someone who doesn't want a favor meeting some other pop star.

Even so, she's been a true friend.

I don't have many of those. I can't afford to lose this one.

CHAPTER ELEVEN
CANCELED

THE MAYFAIR DORMITORY looms ahead, a large gem in the sprawling campus. It could be a postcard of prosperous academia with its red brick and lush ivy, with its arched windows that glint in the setting sun.

Little wonder that this is where the elite reside—the ones who aren't tucked away in the prestigious fraternities and sororities, that is.

As I approach, the automatic doors glide open, revealing a lobby that's more like a five-star hotel than a college dorm. The floors are polished marble, reflecting the soft glow of ornate chandeliers above. Leather sofas and armchairs are arranged in cozy clusters, inviting students to lounge.

The soothing environment doesn't help.

My stomach is in knots.

The air is filled with the scent of fresh flowers,

arranged in vases on the polished wooden tables. Soft classical music plays from hidden speakers, adding to the atmosphere of sophistication.

It's a far cry from Hathaway, where the scholarship kids end up.

Dormitory assignments are supposed to be random, but it never works out that way in real life. There's a lot that never works out like it's supposed to.

When I reach her room, I take a deep breath.

It's just Carlisle. My friend.

I knock on her door, knuckles rapping against the wood in a quick, nervous rhythm. Silence greets me. I wait, wondering if she's studying or napping. Or maybe in class. Study group. There are a million things she could be doing that aren't *waiting to get accused of betrayal by Anne Hill.*

Making this trek again sounds horrible, so I knock again, louder this time. Still nothing. I turn my head and listen. All I hear is the distant hum of voices and the muffled beat of music from down the hall.

I pull out my phone.

Hey, where are you? I'm at your dorm.

I wait, my heart pounding in my ears. But the minutes tick by, and there's no response. Unease grows inside me, even though it means nothing.

She could be in the middle of taking a test right now, her phone safely tucked away. Do they even have tests in music classes? Yes, of course, they must. Though I don't know how they judge her voice, how any of them could possibly tell her that it needs work when millions of people would fill stadiums to hear her sing.

Then again, they probably disdain popularity as much as the literary establishment does. If everyone loves something, then it must somehow be low brow. It must be incomprehensible to be valuable.

The dorm hallway, usually bustling with life, feels eerily quiet.

I check my phone again, hoping to see a reply from Carlisle.

Nothing.

A knot of worry tightens in my stomach.

Which is silly. I didn't tell her I was coming. How could she know? Why would she drop everything to be here? It shouldn't mean anything, except that it's strange to be at class at seven in the evening. It's strange that she's not here precisely when I came to ask her about being the leak to Tanglewood Tea.

It's a coincidence, obviously.

I turn to leave. And hear a soft click behind

me.

Relief washes over me, but it's short-lived. When I turn, instead of Carlisle's familiar face, an older woman in a maintenance uniform appears, headphones tucked into her ears. She's pulling out a cart filled with cleaning supplies, the wheels rattling against the threshold.

My eyes flick up to the empty room behind the woman.

The *very* empty room. The bookshelves are bare, the poster of Mozart that used to hang above her bed is gone. It's like she was never here at all. A cold shiver runs down my spine.

"Excuse me," I say, stepping forward.

The woman looks up, her expression one of boredom and mild annoyance as she tugs her headphones out. "Yes?"

"Do you know where Carlisle went?"

The woman lifts a brow, her gaze sweeping over me.

"I can't say where the students live."

I flush, realizing how this must look—like I'm some obsessed fan trying to track down a celebrity. "Oh, no, I'm not—I'm her friend," I stammer, trying to explain. The words sound hollow, even to my own ears.

The woman gives me a look, one that says

she's heard it before.

"Never mind," I mutter, taking a step back.

The woman shrugs, replacing her headphones and turning back to her cart. I pull out my phone, my fingers flying over the screen as I type out another message to Carlisle.

Hey, did you switch rooms?

No answer, but I notice that my previous message shows as read.

I take a deep breath, trying to calm the churning in my stomach. There has to be a reasonable explanation for all of this. Carlisle wouldn't disappear without a word. Would she? I quicken my pace, the sound of my footsteps echoing off the marble floor.

As I push open the doors to the stairwell, my phone vibrates again. I glance down, my heart leaping into my throat. But it's only a notification from Tanglewood Tea, the latest post popping up on my screen. I follow them in case they have any news on the department takeover, even though many of their posts are about other parts of the university—sports, parties, etc. Anything scandalous. I can't even enjoy the gossip as entertainment, because I know what it's like to be the brunt of it. Each person, no matter how smart or beautiful or far above me they may seem, are humans who are suffering.

Then again, maybe I'm projecting.

Maybe some of them actually like being the source of gossip.

I pause, my finger hovering over the notification. But something stops me from opening it. Andini lives here. Not the man who took over the literature department. His son, Matteo. I remember catching him in a kiss. Remember his snarling anger at being caught in a compromising situation. Modern-day kids don't worry too much about sexual orientation, but parents do. And Matteo's father seems especially stuck in the past.

I also remember which room he was outside of.

Does it belong to the person he was kissing?

Or him?

There's one way to find out.

That feels ballsy, knocking on someone's door, not sure of who's inside. Even if it is Matteo, am I going to confront him about what his father's doing? Am I really that brave?

Apparently I am.

His eyes widen when he opens the door. I see the idea flash through his eyes, the idea of slamming the door in my face. I shove my messenger bag in the space. Try closing it on the five-hundred-page volume of *Art Criticism and Theory*, asshole. He sighs with resignation. "What the hell do you want?"

"To talk."

He sighs, runs a hand through his dark hair. "We can't—"

I step closer, my hands planting firmly on his chest. I push, hard. He stumbles back, allowing me to enter. Though as he steps back, I realize he's too solid to be forced into anything. He let me do it.

I'm close to him, close enough to see the flecks of gold in his brown eyes, the stubble on his jaw. But I don't back down. I won't. "Do you want to explain what your father is doing pretending to be a dean?"

He looks at me, his expression torn. "I can't control him. He wants what he wants, and he won't stop until he gets it."

"And what is it he wants?"

Matteo's eyes close briefly, a pained expression crossing his face. "Power. He wants to shape the future of this university in his image."

Gross. "And you're going to stand by and watch as he destroys everything that makes this place special?"

His eyes flash with a spark of anger. "You

think I want this? You think I want to see my father tear this place apart? It's killing me, too. But I'm helpless. I'm a pawn in his game, the same as you, the same as everyone else."

His voice is raw, filled with a desperation that sends a shiver down my spine. I search his face, looking for any sign of deception, any hint that he's playing me. But all I see is pain, a pain that echoes my own.

"Matteo—" I start, but he cuts me off, his hands coming up to grip my wrists.

"You think I don't see it?" he says, his voice low, intense. "You think I don't see the way he's ruining everything? The way he's using me, using you, using everyone to get what he wants? I see it. And it's tearing me apart."

His grip tightens, his eyes boring into mine. "But I can't stop him. I've tried. I've tried so fucking hard. But he's too strong, too powerful. And I'm just… I'm just his son. I'm just a tool in his game."

His voice breaks, and I see it then, the helplessness in his eyes, the desperation. He's not the enemy, not really. He's another victim, caught in the web of his father's ambition. Like me. Like everyone else. Or is he?

But as I stand there, my heart pounding, my

hands pressed against his chest, I can't help but wonder—is there a way out of this web? A way for us to break free, to fight back? To take control of our own destinies, once and for all?

I hurry down the stairs, my heart pounding in my chest. I pull out my phone, hoping to see a response from Carlisle. But there's nothing.

Only the notification from Tanglewood Tea, taunting me.

I click on it, my breath hitching in my throat as the page loads.

And then I see it.

Carlisle Storm CANCELED. Sources say she's left Tanglewood U in DISGRACE.

I stop dead in my tracks, my heart plummeting. The world around me blurs, the grandeur of Mayfair Dormitory fading into insignificance. I read the post again, the words burning into my mind.

Canceled. Disgrace.

It can't be true. Carlisle, with her bubbly personality and infectious laughter, the one who brought life and light into every room she entered. The one who had the courage to walk away from her celebrity life to pursue her dreams. It can't be true.

But the post is right there, in black and white, the harsh words glaring at me from the screen. I scroll down, my fingers shaking, as I skim through the comments. They're brutal, a mix of gloating and speculation, each one a stab to my heart.

Knew she wouldn't last.

Guess the princess couldn't handle the real world.

What did she do to get kicked out?

I clench my jaw, anger surging through me. I want to scream, to defend her, to tell them they're wrong. But the doubt lingers, a cold, heavy stone in my stomach. Why hasn't she responded to my messages? Why did she leave her dorm room bare, like she never planned to come back?

I look up from my phone, my vision swimming. A group of students walk by, their laughter echoing off the marble floors. They're oblivious to the turmoil inside me, their worlds untouched by the cruel words on the screen. I envy them, their ignorance, their carefree smiles.

I take a deep breath, trying to steady myself.

Is she okay? Of course not.

There's not anything I can do to help, though. Not if she won't respond to me. And certainly being friends with the outcast of notoriety won't help her now-tarnished reputation. How did this happen so quickly? I only saw her a couple of weeks ago. Then again, I know how quickly your life can change.

The sun is setting, casting long shadows across the campus. The beauty of it all seems mocking now, a taunt from a cruel college campus.

CHAPTER TWELVE

Gothic Decay

WHISPERS.

That's what brings me out of sleep.

I remember whispered secrets and desperate kisses. Only, I don't wake up to blue moonlight. Instead there's the yellow sunlight filtering through dusty windows.

Sometime in the middle of the night I made it across campus.

My dorm room.

I'm in my dorm room and hearing whispers.

Is Daisy bringing breakfast again?

Except when I open my eyes, I see two other people in the room. Daisy looks dressed for class while she directs some other young woman—a stranger—to sit on her bed. "I'll be back in a few hours," my roommate whispers.

"What am I supposed to do?" the young woman says.

She has honey-colored hair that's grown long and shimmery with short cropped bangs. The effect emphasizes her round face, making her appear all of twelve, even though she's probably older than that. Especially considering she's in a college dorm room on a Tuesday morning.

"Read a book," Daisy says, gesturing at a stack of textbooks.

"Don't," I manage to say, my voice husky with sleep. "If you aren't required to read physics, I can't imagine why you would."

Daisy doesn't quite manage to hide her wince. She turns to face me with a large, gorgeous smile. Gorgeous enough that I'm sure most people, men and women alike, are awed by it. And distracted.

I recognize her beauty, but I've been her friend long enough to know it's the smile she uses when she's hiding something.

"Good morning," she says brightly.

I raise an eyebrow. "Introduce me to your friend?"

"Oh." She glances back, as if surprised to see a whole person sitting on her narrow twin bed. "This is Mary. She's my…sister."

Holy shit. I sit up, dragging a hand over my face. "Hi, Mary."

"You have a hickey," the not-quite-twelve-year-old says.

A flush heats my face. The memory of William sucking my neck, biting me, while he thrust inside me still feels fresh. "So, are you visiting to take a campus tour?"

She snorts. "As if."

Daisy's overbright smile hasn't wavered. "I'll explain later, but I'm late for class. And if I'm tardy, the professor will use that as an excuse to— never mind," she says at Mary's interested expression. "The important thing is that I'll be back in a few hours. We'll figure it out then."

Then she's gone.

I spare a moment wondering what's going on with her and Professor Stratford. The other Professor Stratford, that is. Then Mary hops off the bed, and I have more pressing problems. Like Mary poking around on our desks, her slender finger and inquisitive blue eyes landing too close to the Shakespeare Society-esque black envelope.

"So," I tell her, my smile no doubt matching Daisy's megawatt version. "Are you hungry? We could go down to the cafeteria."

"Nah, I'm not supposed to be seen."

"Not supposed to be seen?"

"I ran away from home."

"Oh." I wonder if this is one of those harmless

running away from homes that teenagers do, not that I ever did. I would have worried too much about what kind of disaster would have fallen on the house if I had.

Considering Daisy's upbringing, this is probably not regular.

"Will you go back?" I ask, not sure which is the better answer.

"Not unless she makes me," she says, her voice sullen.

"She won't."

It isn't my promise to make, but I can't imagine Daisy making her sister return to that place. Unless it also threatens Daisy's ability to be here. Shit. From the little I know about it, they barely let her come to college, even with the full-ride scholarship. How they could have stopped her isn't something we've gone into detail about, but it sounds like there was abuse.

The idea of this sassy teenager facing pain makes me ache.

She lifts one slender shoulder, as if she feels my silent sympathy and rejects it. "Whatever. I could have gone somewhere else if she didn't want me here. It's not like I can't take care of myself."

I don't want to know how she would take care of herself.

Selling her body?

It's not that I can judge, but I don't want that for her.

"Don't worry," I say. "We'll wait for her to come back."

Mary throws herself into the desk chair, which emphasizes how baggy her jeans really are. Almost falling down, really. They must not belong to her. Exactly how dark and dangerous was this run from her hometown?

Very, most likely.

"So, Mary. Is that like the religious Virgin Mary?"

"Nah. I mean, my dad said that, but he's full of shit. The reality is that our mom was into flowers. That's how she ended up there. She wasn't born into it. They recruited her saying it was a commune, that she could live free, that kind of thing. It wasn't until she had Lily and Clover that she realized it was a trap, I think."

"Oh." What kind of flower…

"Marigold," she says with a roll of her eyes.

I root around in the double buckets under my bed that stand in for a clothes dresser, since it's clear that the option for sleep has passed. "Would you rather I called you Mary?"

"If you want me to answer," she says with an

arch look.

"And how old are you?" The question is a little abrupt, but if Tanglewood policemen are going to burst in here and accuse me of kidnapping, then I should at least know the basics about her.

"Fourteen," she says.

She's short for fourteen. Do they feed them in the cult?

I mean, in the commune?

"Okay," I say, tugging on a pair of jeans beneath my oversized T-shirt that serves as pajamas. "Listen, it's going to be really obvious if there's a random new girl staying in our room. We use the same bathrooms as everyone else on the floor. And we eat in the cafeteria downstairs."

Her expression falls, draining of its spark. "You need me to leave," she says, her voice completely devoid of emotion. "Got it."

"No," I say, fighting down my anger at whatever and whoever made her so practiced at handling someone rejecting her. "I'm saying that I know a place where you'll be safe, where you'll have access to a bathroom and a small kitchen."

"And where is this haven?"

It's across campus, in a place that I've been very recently.

A place where I got this hickey, actually.

I text Daisy letting her know that we're on the move, on the off chance that she gets back early and worries about her. It will be safer to go out now, when the hallways are bustling and no one will ask questions about a random person on our floor. Later at night it will be harder to do that. She'll stand out more with her ill-fitting clothes and her baby face.

She follows me with her head down, glancing up with wide eyes to take in the campus as we pass through. The area around the cathedral is quiet, the bustle of students notably absent. It's just us, and the echo of our hurried footsteps. I set a brisk pace, my heart pounding in my chest, my breath misting in the chilly air.

I can see the fear in her posture, the determination in the set of her chin. She's trusting Daisy, trusting *me*, even though we just met. I won't let her down.

As we approach the bell tower, a sense of unease washes over me.

I've never been here in the daylight.

It looks older and somehow gloomier.

The gothic decay of the building suits the moonlight.

Now, with the sun bouncing off the stained

glass windows of the bell tower, it feels incongruous. Is William watching us? It's only been hours since I left him. He won't expect me. Will he worry that I'm bringing a stranger? He'll probably chastise me for risking exposure, but he also will understand.

He wouldn't let a young girl be in danger, either.

The building looms above us, its stone façade cold and imposing. The heavy wooden door creaks open, the sound echoing through the empty courtyard. I step inside, my eyes adjusting to the dim light.

The bell tower is silent, the air thick with dust and the faint scent of old books. I can hear the distant hum of the campus, but inside, it's like time has stood still. Like we're the only people left in the world.

I lead the way up the winding stone staircase, my footsteps echoing off the cold walls. I can see the tension in her shoulders, the way her hand clenches around the strap of her bag. She's ready for anything, prepared to fight if she has to.

As we reach the top of the staircase, I pause, my heart in my throat. The room is empty, the small cot in the corner gone, leather briefcase missing.

There's no sign of William.

No sign that anyone has been here at all.

Fear grips me, cold and harsh.

Is he safe? Has something happened to him?

The Shakespeare Society could have tracked him here. They could have dragged him out of here and then cleaned up the mess. Although it seems like I would see *something*, if that's what happened.

"What's going on?" The quiver in her voice reveals her age.

I take a deep breath. "I'm not sure."

It's not that reassuring, but I think she'd rather honesty than a lie. "Are we going to pray?"

"What?" Oh God, the cathedral. Of course she'd think me dragging her here had something to do with religion, considering her upbringing. Maybe she thinks the crazy lady is going to make her repent. "No, of course not. This is a good hideout spot. At least I thought it was."

She cocks her head, drawing my attention to a post.

It's one of the posts William used to tie my hands. The rope is still there, thick fibers wrapped around a square beam of wood, bloodred on scarred black walnut. Tucked flush between them is a note.

Had to run. Stay safe. — W

Well. That's a good thing.

At least, it should be good.

Better than a ransom note from the Society, that's for sure. Except it doesn't feel good. It feels terrifying. This cathedral *is* a great hideout spot. And he's gone. Left. He's out there in the world. Now I understand what he meant with his growly threats, why he tied me up and didn't want to release me. Now I understand how hard it is to know that the person you love is at risk.

A small hand curls in mine.

I look down to see Mary providing support, even though she can't understand the scope of it. She understands grief, though. That much I can feel through the gentle weight of her lean, the warmth of her slender body.

"Is it still safe?" she asks.

"Yes," I say, clearing my throat of the worry that's gathered there. "It's still safe. There's a mattress somewhere in the building, most likely. We need to find it. I'll show you the bathroom and the kitchen. There's even a little toaster oven. It's ancient, but it's actually better than we have in the dorm room."

CHAPTER THIRTEEN

Point of No Return

I WAKE TO the soft brush of velvet against my fingertips, a whisper of a touch that stirs me from the depths of sleep. My eyes flutter open. The dim glow of Daisy's string lights casting a warm hue over the room. I look down, my sleepy gaze focusing on the crimson bloom resting on the sheet beside me, its petals soft and full, its scent filling the air with a heady fragrance.

A rose. In my bed.

I bolt upright, my heart pounding in my chest. My eyes dart around the room, searching for any sign of an intruder, but the dorm is quiet, undisturbed.

Daisy's bed is empty, her sheets rumpled, her blanket tossed aside.

She must have stayed with Mary in the bell tower.

I turn back to the rose, my fingers gently

brushing against its petals. It's real, not a dream. But how did it get here? And who could have left it? The answer comes to me in a rush, a wave of heat that sweeps through my body, leaving me breathless.

William. Of course it's him.

How did he get into the dorm? How did he slip past the locked doors, the creaky floors, the thin walls? And why take such a risk?

My mind races, a whirlwind of fear and hope, worry and desire, all tangled together. I press a hand to my chest, feeling the rapid beat of my heart, the rise and fall of my breath.

He was here. In my room.

While I slept.

The thought sends a shiver down my spine, a thrill of something dark and dangerous. He could have done anything, could have taken anything.

But he didn't take anything.

Instead, he left a rose.

A symbol of love, of passion, of promises yet to be fulfilled.

Is love a tender thing? It is too rough,

Too rude, too boist'rous, and it pricks like thorn.

I can almost hear the words spoken in his rumbly voice.

I lift the rose to my nose, inhaling its sweet scent. It's a deep red, the color of blood, of wine, of a rope that used to pull a cathedral bell. It's a reminder of the last night we spent together, the way he claimed me, body and soul.

It's also reckless.

If he's caught, if he's seen, it could ruin everything.

It could risk his life. And mine too.

We're playing with fire, dancing on the edge of a blade. One wrong step, one false move, and we could both get cut. I should be angry at his carelessness. Instead I feel exhilarated, electrified, alive.

I feel like I'm standing on the precipice of something wild and wonderful, something terrifying and thrilling.

I feel like I'm finally, truly awake.

The petals are silky soft beneath the swipe of my thumb.

My phone buzzes from where I left it on my desk.

Did he also find a way to message me?

Slipping out of bed, I keep the rose clutched in my hand. I pad across the room, my bare feet silent on the creaky floorboards. I reach for my phone, my heart pounding in my chest.

Text message from an unknown number.

It's from him. It has to be. Maybe he's telling me the new location where I can find him. I hesitate, my thumb hovering over the icon, because I want it to be him too much. Even though nothing with him has ever been as simple as sending a text message. He embodies the cloak and dagger aspect of the Society.

Then, with a deep breath, I open the message.

It's Professor Thorne.

As I read the words on the screen, my breath catches in my throat. It's a command, a demand, a dare. Most of all, a test.

I stare at the text message, my heart pounding in my chest like a drum.

Be outside your dorm in five minutes. A car will pick you up.

No explanation, no context.

Of course not.

My fingers tighten around the phone, knuckles turning white.

I glance at the rose in my hand, its petals crushed in my anxious fist. William's face flashes through my mind, his eyes dark with desire, his voice a low growl in my ear.

He's not here now.

I'm alone, facing this challenge.

I take a deep breath, steeling myself. I can't

show fear, can't show hesitation. The Society is watching. I have to play this smart, have to keep my cool. I have to make her believe I'm on her side.

It's the only way to get her to trust me so I can ruin her.

It's also the only way for me to stay alive.

Four minutes left.

I quickly pull on a pair of jeans, a sweater, boots. My hands are steady despite the storm raging inside me. I take one last look at the rose, its red petals a stark contrast to the stark white of my bedsheets.

A promise.

And a reminder of what I'm fighting for.

I step out into the cold, the wind whipping around me, biting at my cheeks. I scan the street, my eyes landing on a massive black SUV parked at the curb.

The windows are tinted, the engine running.

A shiver runs down my spine, a mix of fear and revulsion.

The driver's side window rolls down, revealing a man in a dark suit, his eyes hidden behind sunglasses. He doesn't speak, just nods at the back seat.

A command.

I hesitate, my heart pounding in my chest.

This is it, the point of no return. Once I get in that car, there's no going back. I'll be in Thorne's grasp, at her mercy. But I have to take this chance, have to play this game. For William, for myself. He wouldn't want me to get in the car.

Good thing he isn't here, then.

I take a deep breath, my fingers curling around the door handle. I pull it open, the warmth from inside the car spilling out, enveloping me. I slide into the back seat, the leather smooth and cool against my skin. The door clicks shut behind me, the sound echoing in the silence.

The car pulls away from the curb, the engine a low purr. I watch as the campus fades into the distance, the familiar buildings replaced by unfamiliar streets. The car glides to a halt at the edge of a dense forest, the trees towering and bare, their branches like skeletal fingers clawing at the moonlit sky. The cold air bites at my skin, the silence deafening.

What are we doing here?

I wrap my sweater tighter around me, my breath misting in the chill. The driver points toward a faint path leading into the woods.

I hesitate, my heart pounding.

It's time for one of the Society's infamous

pranks, then.

I've always been a bystander in them. Daisy is the one who was hurt. And then Tyler. Even William almost died, though that was more of a murder attempt than a prank. Now it's my turn to experience the full force of the Society.

On some level, maybe I deserve this.

Maybe I really will be initiated into the Society after this.

The forest swallows me whole, the canopy above blocking out the moon, casting everything in eerie shadows. The path is narrow, winding, the trees pressing in on either side. I hear whispers in the rustling leaves, imagine faces in the gnarled trunks.

I round a bend and stumble to a halt, my breath catching in my throat.

Before me is a clearing, bathed in the glow of a roaring fire.

And around the fire, three figures, draped in black cloaks, their faces obscured by hoods. They're chanting, their voices low and haunting, sending a chill down my spine.

"Double, double toil and trouble; Fire burn, and cauldron bubble."

It's the witches' scene from *Macbeth*.

But this isn't a rehearsal. Or even a performance.

This is a ritual, even without magic.

I step back, my instincts screaming at me to run. I'm rooted to the spot, my eyes wide, my heart pounding. The figures don't acknowledge me, just continue their chant, their voices rising, falling, echoing through the forest.

"Scale of dragon, tooth of wolf, Witches' mummy, maw and gulf."

They're adding ingredients to the cauldron, dried leaves with twine, something shriveled that might have been a lizard once. I watch, horrified, fascinated, as they toss in the ingredients. The academic in me has to give them points for accuracy. The rest of me is sickened.

The fire roars higher, the flames licking at the night sky, casting eerie shadows on the trees. The atmosphere is thick, oppressive, the air heavy with the scent of burning herbs, the tang of something metallic.

I can feel the power here, the ambition.

It's chilling me to the bone.

CHAPTER FOURTEEN
Pitch Black

TREES LOOM ABOVE me, their bare branches clacking like skeletal fingers, whispering secrets in the cold wind. I stand rooted to the spot, my heart thudding in my chest, my breath misting in the chill air. This is the Society's doing, their twisted game, and perversely, even though I despise them, I can see the appeal. There's something more *real* about Shakespeare here.

Are the witches students?

They're draped in black cloaks, faces obscured by heavy hoods, moving with a fluid grace around the roaring fire. Their chants fill the air, haunting and melodic, the words winding around me like a spell.

The fire casts eerie shadows, dancing and twisting on the gnarled tree trunks, creating monstrous shapes that seem to reach out for me. The witches toss ingredients into the cauldron—a shriveled root, a vial of dark liquid, a small pouch that rattles with unknown contents. Each addition sends the flames higher, the fire roaring like a wild beast.

I take a deep breath, the cold air stinging my lungs, grounding me. I square my shoulders, lift my chin. I won't be their pawn, their plaything. I've dealt with worse than them—my parents' abuse, their lies, their cruelty. I've survived, grown stronger. I can face whatever the Society throws at me.

The chanting stops abruptly, the sudden silence deafening.

The witches turn to me, their faces still hidden by dark hoods, their bodies bent as if they're really old crones. Anticipation hangs heavy in the air. I steel myself, ready for whatever comes next. I won't back down, won't show weakness. This is their game, their test. And I'm ready to play.

One of the witches steps forward, her cloak billowing behind her like a dark cloud. She extends a hand, a small, intricately carved wooden box resting on her palm. Her voice, when she speaks, is low, husky, laced with a power that seems to vibrate in the air. "Open it," she commands, her eyes glinting in the firelight.

I hesitate, my heart pounding. Whatever's in

that box, it's not going to be pleasant. But I can't refuse. I reach out, my fingers brushing against hers as I take the box. Her skin is ice cold, sending a jolt up my arm. I take a deep breath, my thumb tracing the carvings on the lid.

The box is heavier than it looks, the wood dark and smooth under my fingers. I trace the intricate carvings, feeling the grooves like a secret language against my skin.

The witches watch me, their eyes gleaming in the firelight, their bodies tense with anticipation. Nestled in velvet, the color of midnight, is a dagger.

It's not just any dagger—it's a work of art, a tribute to violence. The hilt is gilded, adorned with jewels that wink malevolently in the firelight. A ruby the size of my thumb sits at the pommel, surrounded by a circle of obsidian stones that seem to absorb the light.

The blade is thin, wickedly sharp, with a groove running down the center, designed, I know from a research paper I read once, to make the blood flow faster. This isn't a prop, a plaything.

This is a weapon meant for killing.

I recoil, my hands shaking.

The box clatters to the ground, the dagger

falling onto the dirt.

The fire roars, the flames reaching higher, as if fed by my fear.

The witches step closer, their cloaks billowing, their faces still hidden. I can feel their eyes on me, their excitement, their hunger. This is what they wanted, what they craved—my shock, my terror.

"What do you want from me?" I ask, my voice shaking only slightly.

No answer. Only the crackle of the fire, the rustle of the leaves, the distant hoot of an owl. The witches circle me, their movements fluid, predatory. I feel like prey, like a rabbit surrounded by wolves. My heart hammers in my chest, my breath coming in short, sharp gasps. I'm in way over my head, drowning in a game I don't understand, a game with rules I never knew.

"Pick it up."

The witch's command still hangs in the air, the small box heavy in my hands. Before I can make sense of its contents, a rustling sound echoes through the forest. The witches turn in unison, their cloaks billowing like dark wings. My heart hammers in my chest, my breath hitches. What now?

Branches snap. Leaves crunch.

And then, suddenly, Brandon is dragged into

the clearing, his arms gripped tightly by two more cloaked figures. His usually perfectly styled dark blond hair is disheveled, his brown eyes wide with fear. My stomach drops, a cold dread washing over me. This is bad. Really bad.

He struggles, trying to get free, but the figures hold him tight.

His eyes dart around the clearing, taking in the fire, the witches, me. When his gaze lands on me, he freezes, his eyes widening in disbelief. "Anne?" His voice is a choked whisper, filled with fear and confusion.

I'm rooted to the spot, my mind racing.

He cheated on me when we were dating. He insulted me when I was with his father. Then he turned his back on me when I wanted closure.

Despite everything, I don't want him to be hurt.

"What are you doing here?" I whisper.

He swallows hard, his eyes flicking to the witches, then back to me. "They took me from my dorm. I don't know what's going on, but it's not good."

That's an understatement.

I look at the witches, their faces still obscured, their bodies tense. This is a test, a sick game. They want to see what I'll do, how far I'll go. I clench my jaw, my resolve hardening. I won't let them use Brandon to get to me.

I won't let them win.

"Let him go," I say.

The witches don't move, their grip on Brandon tightening. He flinches.

One of the witches steps forward, her voice a low hiss. "Kill him."

My stomach churns, bile rising in my throat. The witch's words hang heavy in the air, a death sentence echoing through the forest. I look at Brandon, his eyes wide with terror, the charm replaced by a raw, primal fear.

Fuck. They want me to prove my loyalty, to show that I'm one of them. In doing so, I'll also give them the strongest blackmail they could have against me. I would be their puppet forever. Even if I were willing to hurt another student, it would be a devil's bargain. Of course, I'm not willing to do it either way.

I won't let them use Brandon as a pawn.

Won't let them control me.

Won't let them hurt William Stratford through his son.

The witches circle us, their chants filling the air, a haunting melody that sends shivers down my spine. The fire roars, the flames licking higher, casting eerie shadows on the gnarled trees. The cauldron bubbles, the liquid inside churning, spitting, hissing like a living thing. It's an important reminder. Because I'm not superstitious, but I do love Shakespeare.

Which means I know what's in that cauldron, if they were accurate.

As I once told Professor Thorne, humans cause enough evil without magic.

My gaze flicks over the pile of ingredients. Some questionable looking herbs. Some dark apothecary bottles that might hold anything, really. And there…yes. Some alcohol. Something high-proof, I hope. Their stunts have only gotten more dangerous, and more dramatic, since the masquerade I first attended. But these people still like to get drunk, to gamble, and have sex. And if they used the actual ingredients from the play, there are several flammable ones.

I take a step forward Brandon, holding the knife. His eyes widen.

A blink. It's all the warning I can give him.

He stares at me, his brown eyes so like his father. And I think he understands?

Though there's no time to find out. I make a dash for the pile. Before they can grab me, I smash the bottle against the heavy iron rim of the cauldron. Flames roar from the mouth. With my foot, I kick the hot container over, letting the boiling liquid pour toward them. There's screaming. Someone grabs my arm, and I flail, fighting them, until I hear Brandon's voice in my ear, "It's me."

We run together, dashing deeper into the woods, hearing cursing and shouts behind us. We keep running, my breath unbearably loud in the empty woods. It feels like a red flare, as if they're sure to catch up, to find us, to murder us both.

My lungs burn from the exertion.

And then my legs.

And still we keep running.

Finally we reach some edge of the woods, a break into a long, winding road.

We both stop, bent over. I gasp for breath.

It feels like it's only been a few seconds since we started running, but the stitch in my side says it's been longer. I haven't heard them in a long time. I glance back. "I hope it doesn't set the entire woods on fire."

Brandon looks back. "Unlikely. Though it would serve them right to get caught in it."

"You know what just occurred to me? What they did back there, the costumes, the chanting. It was technically a performance. And it turned out pretty bad. Maybe the play *is* cursed."

He looks blank. "What?"

"You really never cared about Shakespeare, did you?"

"No, and after this, I'm never reading another play again. I don't care what my mom says, I'm never going to read another fucking old word again. I'm going to become a finance stockbroker dudebro who makes a shit ton of money."

That makes me smile. "Good."

"I think campus is that way," he says, pointing with his thumb.

It's pitch black. "How can you tell?"

"I was a boy scout for ten years."

"How did I not know that about you?"

He shrugs, and even in the darkness, he looks like he might be blushing. Or maybe that's just the exertion of running for miles to save your life. "I guess I didn't really open up to you. I mostly wanted to show you off to my friends and then make out. I was pretty shallow."

"Well, you're planning to be a dudebro. That's kind of a prerequisite."

"Thanks for not killing me."

"Yeah, well."

"It would have made things awkward for you and my dad, that's for sure."

"It's already awkward, what with him being dead."

Brandon raises his hands. "He told me I couldn't say anything."

"That pisses me off, that neither of you trusted me."

We start down the road for the long, long walk.

"I think he trusted you," he finally says. "He was trying to protect you."

I roll my eyes. "Right."

"Man, I don't know why I'm arguing for him. He stole my girl."

"We weren't together," I remind him. "Because you cheated on me. And besides, you should be on his side. He cares about you. It's part of why he took the job at the university, so that he could spend time with you."

"I know they used me to get to him. My mom helped them."

A pang in my chest. "I'm sorry."

"Families are fucked up."

"Yeah. Families are fucked up."

CHAPTER FIFTEEN

Scholarship Fund

"WHAT IS THE difference between a king and a tyrant?"

Professor Thorne waits quietly in the large classroom. She doesn't quite look at me, but I can feel her waiting. Plotting. I'm in danger every moment I sit here. Part of me wants to run away. The other part knows that I have nowhere to go.

Tanglewood University was my only sanctuary.

I'll make my stand here.

The Society will come after me, of course.

It's the morning after the fire. Probably I'll be carried off in a dark hood in a white van, made the subject of one of its violent little stunts as retribution for the one I ruined in the forest. Someone will have to cut off my head; maybe the same way Malcolm does to Macbeth. Either that or it will be a soulless, modern killing.

I'm not even sure which one is worse.

A few people have raised their hands.

Thorne casually flicks her manicured fingers at one of them.

"Duncan is referred to as a king, because he shows bounty, perseverance, and mercy. While Macbeth is considered a tyrant due to his violent temperament."

She doesn't even grace the student with a glance. "What a very, very…literal interpretation. Yes, that is what the text says. What does it mean?"

A couple of the hands fall, not wanting her disdain.

Though several brave souls keep their hands in the air. This is a senior-level class, after all. They know they'll face worse criticism and derision than that, if they want to share their ideas once they graduate.

Academia eats its own.

"Matteo," she snaps, and he straightens in his seat.

There's a long enough pause to make people shift in their seats, wondering if he will even answer her. The golden boy looks distinctly discouraged today, eyes on his blank desk. Finally he says, "Ambition."

Thorne's lids lower. "Keep going."

"He committed murder to attain the throne. It would always be tainted after that. And more than that, it would never be enough. Because he knew he hadn't earned the crown, so he could never be satisfied with it."

My heart gives a hard kick.

A murmur runs through the classroom.

Most of them know the rumors surrounding the Tempest Prize. The way that my essay originally scored highest until they became suspicious of my professor writing the essay for me.

A well-placed whisper in someone's ear.

And a thick donation to the foundation's bank account.

Then suddenly second place won instead. It was Matteo's essay, but it was Thorne who got accolades for mentoring the winning student. Ironic that she probably did write his essay, when I wrote my own. Funny how narcissists give themselves away by accusing people of their own crimes.

Thorne smiles, her beautiful face grim. "In that case, do you think he welcomed beheading in the end?"

Matteo meets her eyes, his energy, even sitting

in the small, uncomfortable seats, one of intensity. "Maybe, if it was his only way out."

"How perverse," she says with a small laugh. "Maybe Ms. Hill can tell us how it feels to have a sword hanging over her neck."

Everyone's face swings to me.

I could shrug. Or maybe walk out. None of it will really change my fate.

Which gives me a form of freedom.

"It feels like the truth," I say. "Like finally being honest, even if it means you have to die. Nothing less than that is worth living for, anyway."

Her eyes narrow. I feel her wrath whip around my ankles like cold, wintry air. She stands, and I wonder almost idly if she plans to be violent in the classroom. With Andini at the helm, she'll probably get away with it.

Suddenly, the door slams open.

Dean Blake Morris steps through, his silhouette framed by the harsh fluorescent lights of the hallway. He looks like he's been through hell and back. Not only because of the vicious scar that always mars his handsome face. Also because of the fire that blazes in his eyes. He wears the same suit that another dean might, but he doesn't look like an academic. Not right now, anyway.

He looks fierce, powerful, like a warrior ready for battle.

I sit up straighter, my hands gripping the desk. *What's happening?*

He strides forward, his steps echoing in the now-silent classroom.

Thorne struggles to find her voice. "Why, Mr. Morris. Good morning."

"That's Dean Morris to you. Or at least, that's what you can call me for the next second you're still working here."

She gapes. "What is the meaning of this?"

"You're fired."

"You can't just—"

"There's been a change in management. You know all about those, don't you?" A man and woman follow Dean Morris inside, remaining stationed by the door. They're wearing the uniform of campus police. "They will escort you out, to make sure you don't try to steal the silver on the way out."

Thorne's expression is torn between humiliation and imperious fury. In the end, she decides to lift her chin and walk out. The police officers follow, closing the door behind them.

Dean Morris moves to the podium, addressing the class.

"Effective immediately, Luca Andini and Professor Isolde Thorne have been removed from their positions at Tanglewood University."

A collective gasp ripples through the crowd. Murmurs erupt, a wave of relief and confusion crashing against the silence.

"I've been reinstated," he says, his voice deep and resonating. "They tried to silence me. They tried to silence us, but they failed."

There's something electric in the air, a spark of rebellion igniting in the hearts of every student present.

"They think they can control us using fear and manipulation," he continues, his voice steady, his gaze unyielding. "But we have something stronger here at Tanglewood University. We have the truth."

A cheer erupts. Someone slaps me on the back. I'm in shock, numb underneath the confusion. It's…over? It doesn't feel over. It feels like they're lurking underneath the desks, outside the sunshine-y window.

Maybe it will always feel like this, the way that soldiers jump at the sound of fireworks. Maybe Dean Morris knows about that. He used to be in the military, after all, before he began his career as a professor of classical history.

Dean Morris puts up a hand, gradually quitting the tidal wave of support and solidarity. "We have exposed their corruption. We have taken back what's ours. And we will bring those responsible to justice."

His words are a battle cry, a call to arms that resonates deep within me. I feel a surge of emotion—anger, determination, hope—all intertwined, all burning bright and hot in my chest.

Dean Morris takes a deep breath, his expression softening slightly as he looks out at the crowd. "But it will be a long road. They managed to damage many things here in the department in their short tenure. We have uncovered evidence of gross misconduct, of financial impropriety, and of actions that put our students in harm's way. News of those things will come out in the next few weeks, which will also tarnish Tanglewood University's reputation."

My hands tremble, and I clench them tighter, nails digging into my palms. I knew about the Society's stunts, of course, having been involved in one myself quite recently. I'm concerned about other misconduct, about financial impropriety. Surely the university won't have to close or anything drastic? Surely there are checks and balances in place to keep that from happening?

"I know you're scared. I know you're angry, not only at them, but at those in power who should have known better. Those who should have protected you. Including myself. I knew when I left to protect my family that I would leave you undefended, even though I also worked to make it temporary. I'm sorry for that. I also know that you are strong. And though you shouldn't have to be, you are resilient. You are the heart and soul of this university. And together, we will overcome this."

His words are a balm, soothing the raw edges of my fear, my uncertainty. I feel a sense of resolve settling over me, a steely determination.

"I want to be clear," Dean Morris says, his voice rising, his gaze sweeping over the crowd. "This is not the end. This is the beginning. The beginning of a new era at Tanglewood University. An era of transparency, of accountability, of integrity. An era where the safety and well-being of our students come first. Always."

The classroom erupts into a chaotic symphony of voices, students chattering loudly as they gather their things and begin to file out. I'm still glued to my seat, my mind a whirlwind of disbelief and uncertainty. Eventually, I manage to pick up my bag and stand, my legs feeling like they might buckle beneath me.

Dean Morris calls out, "Ms. Hill, a moment, please."

I walk over to him, my heart pounding in my chest like a drum. He waits until the last of the students filter out, leaving us alone in the now-silent classroom.

"How are you doing?" he asks, his voice gentle yet firm.

"Fine," I reply, the word automatic, hollow.

He nods, seeing right through me. "I need to talk to you about something," he says, his expression growing serious. "As I mentioned earlier, there's more coming out in the next few weeks. Specifically about the scholarship fund."

Dread settles in my stomach, a heavy stone sinking deeper and deeper. "What about it?" I ask, my voice barely above a whisper.

He pauses, choosing his words carefully. "It's been drained."

Not stolen from, not reduced. *Drained.*

I stare at him, the words echoing in my mind, their implications crashing over me like a tidal wave. How could that be? What does that mean for me? For Daisy? For all the students who rely on that fund to make their education possible?

"I don't understand," I manage to choke out. "How could that happen?"

He shakes his head, a grim look in his eyes. "We're still investigating. But it seems that Thorne and Andini were able to siphon funds using fake student profiles. They were careful, covering their tracks."

I feel a surge of anger, hot and fierce.

Just as quickly, I deflate.

Maybe the grief process is supposed to take time, but it feels like seconds.

"So, what now?" I ask, my voice hollow. "What happens to us?"

"You're covered for the rest of the semester. Those bills were paid months ago. But next semester, your last semester? I won't lie to you, Ms. Hill. They moved the money offshore, so it will be tricky to get it back. It probably won't happen by January when tuition and housing is due. But I promise you, we *will* fix this. The department will make this right."

I nod, trying to absorb his words, trying to find comfort in them. But the dread in my stomach remains, a gnawing fear that whispers, what if they can't? What if it's too late? I'm not meant to go to college in five years or however long it takes to get money back from overseas.

How will I even live in the meantime?

"I wanted to tell you in person, so that you know that, whatever you hear in the news, we're going to fix this. You have my word."

I meet his gaze, seeing the determination in his eyes. And for a moment, I allow myself to believe him. To hope. "Thank you, Dean Morris. I'm glad that you're okay. And that your family is okay?"

The question comes out higher pitched at the end, as if it's a question. I remember the sunny smile of his wife in the photo on his desk, the two chubby-cheeked children, and my pulse speeds up.

His brown eyes warm. "They're safe. I had to make sure they were protected before I could truly fight for the school."

"I'm glad," I tell him honestly.

There's no anger, that he should have put us first. Of course his wife and two small kids are his highest priority. That's how a family should work. I know that, even if I've never really been part of one.

As I walk out of the classroom, the weight of his words presses down on me, a crushing burden that leaves me wondering, what now? What happens next for a broke kid from Port Lavaca?

Because my parents have never made sure I was safe, have never protected me, not once. I've taken every step on my own, fought for every single thing I've ever done.

Perhaps I should keep fighting.

Isn't that what he said in the classroom?

But I'm just so tired. So tired of fighting, of struggling, of always having to be strong. I want the luxury, the privilege, the someday-dream of getting to be weak, for even a moment.

Maybe that's what Macbeth felt as the sword fell.

Maybe he knew he'd finally get to rest.

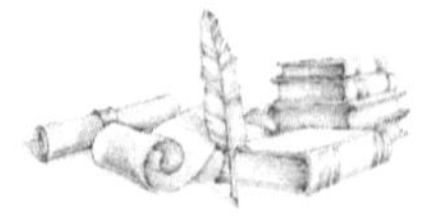

CHAPTER SIXTEEN

Fallout Central

I WAKE UP with a start, the early morning light filtering through the grimy window of my dorm room. My heart hammers in my chest as fragments of last night's events come rushing back.

The forest, the witches, Brandon. A nightmare.

I sit up, my breath coming in quick gasps, and scan the room. Daisy's bed is still empty. I'm guessing she stayed the night with Mary, because she wasn't here when I went to bed.

Which is just as well.

I'd have had to tell her the truth. She would have seen the tragedy on my face, anyway. So better that she slept another night thinking she still had an education, room and board, an entire future ahead of her.

I swing my legs out of bed, the cold floor

sending a shiver up my spine. Bracing myself, I pad over to the window, peering out at the campus below. There's a vibrant energy in the air, a vague sense of commotion. Students are gathered in small clusters, their heads bent together, whispering.

The news is breaking.

I pull on a hoodie over my pajamas, not bothering to change, and slip out of my room, the hallway eerily quiet. The usual chatter of back-and-forth students is absent, replaced by a tense hum. I make my way toward the common room.

As I walk, the murmur of voices grows louder.

I round the corner and freeze. The common area is filled with students, their faces etched with worry and fear. They huddle together, their eyes darting around the room, their voices hushed.

I step out into the hallway, the din of voices growing louder. Students cluster in tight groups, their faces flushed with excitement and worry.

Lorelei, our usually stern resident advisor, is at the center of it all, her voice brisk and commanding as she tries to restore order. "Everyone, calm down," she snaps, her eyes scanning the crowd. "There are too many people here. It's against the fire code. Some of you go back to your rooms."

Her words do little to quell the chaos. The air

is electric, buzzing with an energy that's almost palpable. I push my way through the throng, catching snippets of conversation.

"Did you see the post?"

"Can you believe it?"

"What's going to happen now?"

I spot a girl I recognize from my Latin class, her eyes wide as she stares at her phone. I tap her shoulder. "What's going on?"

"Tanglewood Tea just dropped a major exposé. It's all about Luca Andini and the Shakespeare Society. It's…it's huge."

She shoves her phone in my face, and I allow myself to take it, handling the piece of metal as if it's a live snake. It's opened to a series of social media posts that contain text instead of images.

It's all there, in stark black and white. The corruption, the bribes, the manipulation. Will this be enough to bring them down for good?

Or will they find a way to spin this, to twist it to their advantage?

I hand the phone back, my mind racing. Lorelei is still trying to herd everyone back into their rooms, her voice growing hoarse with the effort. But no one is listening. They're all too caught up in the drama.

And the fallout.

That's us, fallout central.

It won't matter to my college career if the Society takes the school back.

I won't be able to take classes or live in the dorm. The area around the university, and most of Tanglewood, would cost too much for me to get an apartment for long, except in the most unsafe areas.

Does that mean I'm moving back home?

Does it mean I'm going to need a permanent position at the diner?

I press my back against the cool wall of the hallway, the chatter of my peers fading into a dull hum as my heart starts to race. The air feels thin, like I can't quite catch my breath. I close my eyes, trying to focus, to steady myself, but the darkness only makes it worse.

"Are you okay?" A voice cuts through the fog, but I can't quite place it. I open my eyes, the hallway spinning slightly. I see a girl from down the hallway, the one who's always shaving in the bathroom. No matter what time of day it is, shaving. Right now her brows furrowed with concern.

Are you okay?

I try to speak, but the words get stuck in my throat. I nod instead, a jerky motion that feels disconnected from my body. She doesn't look convinced but gets pulled away by the current of the crowd.

The walls feel like they're closing in.

I burst into my dorm room, the door slamming shut behind me.

My scholarship. The only reason I'm able to attend Tanglewood. The only way I have to escape Port Lavaca, to escape my parents, to build a future for myself. I feel the color drain from my face, my body suddenly numb.

Daisy bursts into our dorm room, her cheeks flushed, blonde hair disheveled. She must have run all the way here. Her blue eyes meet mine, wide and worried. "Where have you been? I've been trying to reach you."

"I've been right here. In this room. That we share."

Her brows lower in confusion. "Why are you in bed?"

"I've decided to quit school and run away with the circus."

"Did you see the *Daily Tangle*?"

"No, but I can guess what it says."

Daisy paces the length of our cramped dorm room, her blonde hair a mess from running her fingers through it. She clutches her phone, the screen displaying the homepage of the *Daily Tangle*, which is the university's award-winning college newspaper. It's pretty good, but Tanglewood Tea definitely got the scoop on them this time.

"Luca Andini stole millions. *Millions* of the university's dollars."

"Actually, they were our dollars." I've had more time to process this, to wrap my head around it. Daisy, on the other hand, is still in shock, her blue eyes wide with disbelief.

"No one knows where he is. Some people are saying he left the country."

"Friends, Romans, countrymen, lend me your ears; I come to bury my diploma, not to graduate."

"Thorne made a statement," Daisy continues, her voice shaking. "She tried to distance herself from Andini, saying she's just one of his victims. Unfortunately they caught her signature on some of the documents."

"Good." I can't help but feel a twinge of satisfaction at that. Thorne deserves to squirm under the weight of her own lies.

"I can't believe this is happening," Daisy says, sinking down onto her own bed, her shoulders slumped. "What are we going to do, Anne?"

I shrug, the gesture feeling hollow. "I told you about my circus plans."

Daisy looks up at me, her eyes narrowing. "Be serious, Anne. Our scholarships…our futures…it's all up in the air now. We need a plan."

This was my plan. Plan A, B, and C.

The scholarship fund was my lifeline, my ticket out of Port Lavaca, away from my parents, away from that stifling small-town life. And now, it's been ripped away, stolen by a man who was already rich. The injustice of it all burns in my chest, a hot flame.

"I don't know," I admit, my voice barely above a whisper.

I think of the other students, the ones who rely on that money to be here, to chase their dreams. What will happen to them? To us? Will we be forced to drop out, to leave Tanglewood and all the possibilities it holds? The thought makes me sick, a churning in my gut that won't go away.

Daisy looks up at me. "I don't know what to feel."

I shake my head, trying to put my turbulent emotions into words. "I do. It's angry. I thought Tanglewood was different, that the scholarship could level the playing field. Turns out that was a lie."

"I'm going to throw up."

"Try to do it so that it leaves a stain. We should make our mark before we have to move out of here."

"How can you be so glib?"

I think of Luca Andini, of his smug smile and his expensive suits. Of the way he wields his power, like a weapon, cutting down anyone who gets in his way. "I don't know. I'm still trying to wrap my head around all of this too."

Her phone chimes, and she looks down at it, her brow furrowing. "There's an email from the bursar's office. They're setting up meetings with the students. All of us are getting links to book one."

I nod, a sense of dread washing over me. They're only going to tell me what Dean Morris already did. That it will take time. "Sounds fun."

Daisy looks up at me, her eyes filled with worry. "We'll figure this out. Together. Right?"

I force a smile, even as I feel a sense of numbness spreading through me. "Right. Together." But even as I say the words, I can't shake the feeling of helplessness that's settled over me. The feeling that our futures are spinning out of control, and there's nothing we can do to stop it.

"We'll figure this out. You'll see."

I wish I had her optimism, but all I can see is the uncertain future stretching out before us, a future that's as dark and tangled as the woods that surround Tanglewood.

I start to pack, my movements mechanical, my mind racing. But no matter how fast my thoughts spin, I can't see a way out of this. I can't see a future where Daisy and I aren't forced to leave Tanglewood, to leave the life we've built here.

And that thought is more terrifying than anything else.

CHAPTER SEVENTEEN

911

I WAKE UP with a start, the sunlight streaming through the window, casting a harsh glare on the reality that comes crashing down on me. My heart pounds in my chest, my breath coming in short gasps as the realization hits me like a freight train.

The thoughts race through my mind, a whirlwind of emotions and implications that leave me reeling. How did I not see it before? The pieces fit together so perfectly, the subtle hints, the insider knowledge, the way the posts seemed to echo the sentiments of someone I knew.

Carlisle.

The name echoes in my mind, a bitter taste on my tongue.

Holy shit.

Betrayal stings, a sharp pain that reaches deep inside.

I thought she was my friend. How could she have done this?

No, I have to be wrong.

Except…I think I'm not.

I trusted her, shared my secrets, my fears, my dreams. And all this time, she was hiding behind a screen, using my life, our lives, as fodder for her gossip account.

The anger surges within me, a hot, fierce emotion that threatens to consume me. I clench my fists, my nails digging into my palms, the physical pain a welcome distraction from the turmoil within. I want to scream, to shout, to demand answers, to make her see the pain she's caused.

But beneath the anger, there's a sense of hurt, of loss. The realization that our friendship was built on lies, that the trust I placed in her was misguided. The memories of our shared laughter, our late-night talks, our plans for the future—they all seem tainted now, marred by the knowledge of her deception.

I take a deep breath, the air shuddering in my lungs as I try to calm the storm within me. I need to think, to plan, to decide what to do with this knowledge. The implications are vast, the potential for destruction immense. Tanglewood

Tea has the power to make or break reputations, to expose secrets, to shatter lives.

I reach for my phone, my fingers trembling as I type out a single message.

I know what you did.

The words stare back at me, stark and accusatory, a declaration of war. I hesitate for a moment, my thumb hovering over the send button, the weight of the action pressing down on me. But then I think of the pain, the betrayal, the lies.

I delete them and type again. *Call me. 911.*

And press send.

I wait, my heart pounding, my breath coming in short gasps, for the explosion that is sure to follow. The silence is deafening, the wait agonizing, as I stare at the screen, willing a response to appear.

I'm not sure what I expect, what I want, what I need. An explanation? An apology? A denial? A confession? The possibilities swirl in my mind, leaving me dizzy and disoriented.

My phone buzzes almost instantly, Carlisle's name flashing across the screen. I pick up, my heart pounding in my chest, the anger and hurt bubbling just beneath the surface.

"Anne," Carlisle says, her voice breathless,

urgent.

"I know you're Tanglewood Tea," I say, my voice steady, firm, despite the turmoil within me. "I know you've been using me, using us, for your gossip column. I know that you're the reason why William Stratford almost died."

There's a pause, a moment of silence that stretches out between us, heavy with the weight of the accusation. Then, finally, she speaks, her voice soft, resigned.

"I'm not going to deny it," she says.

Tears of frustration and hurt spring to my eyes. I didn't want it to be true. I wait, the anger simmering, the hurt burning, for her to explain, to justify, to make me understand.

"But I never wanted to hurt anyone. It started off as a joke."

"My life is a joke to you?"

"It was a joke about *me*. God, the way people followed me, taking photos, not even having the decency to pretend to be doing a selfie or reading on their phones, just holding it up, snap-snap-snapping, trying to get the best shot so they could post it."

"I was there for some of it," I say, having seen it on the campus tour.

"I know. That's why I—" A small, halted

sound. A sob?

My heart clenches. "Carlisle—"

"No, I need to explain. You deserve that much."

"Yes. I do."

"I wrote a post about me, how vapid I am, how vain. How much of a joke it was for me to be at Tanglewood University, a real place of academia, when I was just a pop singer who relies on glitter and Auto-Tune to be popular."

"That's bullshit," I say, more resigned than protective. Her voice is like an angel. Even pissed at her, I can admit that.

"I couldn't even know if that's how I got admitted, because of my actual talent or because of my fame. I wasn't like you and Daisy, who are coming on full scholarships because you beat out thousands of people for those spots."

My stomach clenches. The scholarship was a gift. It felt deserved…and also, not deserved. Because I shouldn't get an education at the expense of someone else. The entire system is set up as some kind of dark academia Hunger Games.

"I took a photo of me at my worst, looking faux glamorous. And I wrote a post that was real but also fake. I published it under the most ridiculous name I could think of. Nothing happened for a week. I forgot about it. Then I guess someone found it. It got shared and shared and shared. I thought about taking it down."

"Why didn't you?"

"Because it was real, somehow."

I shake my head, not quite understanding but also not refuting it. She's never lived with my problems, but I've never lived with hers. "It sounds masochistic."

A short, bubbly laugh from over the line, and it feels like we're friends again.

Then the smile fades from my lips.

"Yes," she says. "It probably was. I didn't post that often at first, only when I wanted to make fun of myself. Then I saw this kid on the football team get away with roofie-ing some girl's drink, and I posted about it. And it grew into something bigger than myself, something huge… Something I didn't always control."

I listen, the anger slowly ebbing, replaced by a sense of confusion, of uncertainty. I think of the posts, the stories, the secrets exposed. The pain, the humiliation, the destruction. But also, the honesty—the raw, unfiltered reality of our lives.

"Did you control it when you posted about me?" I ask, the hurt seeping through.

"I'm sorry," she says, her voice heavy with

regret. "I'm so sorry. I never meant for them to out your name, but I was worried about you. People started sending tips to the Tanglewood Tea account. I heard about a professor and a student—and I remembered what you said to me. I thought he was taking advantage of you, using you when you were desperate to stay at the school, when you had no choice but to do what he said."

That's why she was so sure that the account hadn't used my name. She'd been the one to write the post. I take a deep breath, the emotions swirling, the pain and the anger and the confusion all mixing, all merging, all blending into one. "You may not have meant for my name to get doxed, but that's what happened."

"I know," she whispers.

"Is that why you called your fancy PR person? Because of guilt?"

"Yes," she says, her voice hollow. "Partly, but also because I care about you. I still care about you. I hope you can forgive me. Please."

"I… I have to think about it."

A pause. "Okay. That's fair."

The call ends, the silence echoing, the void stretching out before me. I sit there, the phone clutched in my hand, the reality of the conversation, of the confession, of the truth, all sinking in, all settling, all seeping into the very core of my being.

And as I sit there, the emotions swirling, the thoughts racing, the pain and the anger and the confusion all merging, all blending, all becoming one, I realize that the path forward is uncertain, the future unclear, the decisions yet to be made.

I sit on the edge of my bed, the mattress sagging beneath me, the silence of the dorm room pressing in on all sides. The posters on the walls, the books on the shelves, the clothes strewn across the floor, all of it so familiar, so normal, so mundane. But it all feels different now, tainted, a façade of happiness and security that's been stripped away, revealing the ugly truth beneath.

The truth is that I never belonged here.

I thought Tanglewood University was my salvation, my escape from the hell of Port Lavaca, from the abuse and the lies. From the pain. I thought the campus was the promise of a brighter future. Now it seems like a cruel joke.

And then there's Carlisle, my friend, my confidante. My betrayer.

A pang of loss settles in my chest, a hollow space where trust had been. I thought I had found a friend, someone who accepted me, who cared about me. Maybe she *did* care about me, as she says, but I'm too confused to understand it right now.

Especially coming on the heels of the news about the scholarship. It's as if the entire university is expelling me, the way a body pushes a foreign body out.

I never really belonged here.

That's why I have to leave.

I look down at my hands, at the fingers that touched Professor Stratford, that felt the heat of his skin, that gripped the sheets in ecstasy and in agony. I think about the choices I've made, the risks I've taken, the boundaries I've blurred from the very first night at the Pinnacle. It was all so I could stay.

This dorm room was once my home.

Now it's a relic of a past life.

I reach for my suitcase, tucked away under my bed, and haul it out. The zipper protests as I yank it open, the sound echoing in the quiet room. I begin to pack, my movements mechanical, detached, like I'm an automaton that Daisy built. Clothes, books, toiletries—each item a piece of the life I'm leaving behind.

As I pack, I search for the emotions inside me.

Anger. Sadness. They should be there.

Instead, I feel empty.

I can't stay here, not anymore. Not after everything I've lost.

Tanglewood is no longer a sanctuary.

I need to leave.

Not only the school, the city.

I'm leaving Stratford, along with the love, the passion, the heartache he represents. I'm leaving it all behind, stepping into the unknown, embracing the future, whatever it may hold. Maybe I can join Daisy's cult. *Hello, God. It's me, the college dropout.*

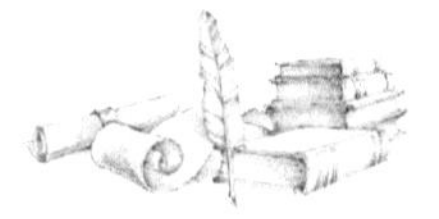

CHAPTER EIGHTEEN

Room and Board

THE DOOR TO my dorm room swings open, the sudden draft making pages on the desk flutter. I jump, my heart leaping into my throat, as Professor William Stratford steps into the room. His presence fills the small space, making it seem tiny. It's a little mouse hole. He's the lion. I'm the mouse in this scenario.

His gaze lands on the packed suitcase on my bed, the open drawers, the emptied desk. His jaw clenches, a muscle twitching in his cheek.

His eyes, intense and stormy, lock on to mine. "What the hell are you doing?"

I straighten, steeling myself against the on-slaught of emotions that always come at the sight of him. Frustration, sadness, longing—they all war within me, making it hard to breathe, hard to think, hard to speak. "What does it look like I'm doing?"

He closes the door behind him. And locks it.

Ominous, that.

I wish I could pretend that I mind more than I actually do.

I wish I didn't want one last kiss. It will have to last a lifetime.

"You can't leave," he says, his voice a command, a demand, a plea.

I bristle at his words, at the assumption that he can tell me what to do. "Watch me," I say, though I can't deny that it feels like foreplay. I turn back to packing, shoving a stack of clothes into my threadbare duffel bag with more force than necessary.

He crosses the room in two long strides, his fingers brushing my wrist, stopping me mid-motion. His touch is electric, sending a jolt of awareness through me, a reminder of the passion we shared, the love that lingers despite everything. "I fought for you," he says, his voice low. "I fought for *us*. Now I've won, and you're leaving?"

I wrench away from him, the sudden absence of his touch leaving me feeling bereft. "You won," I say, my voice shaking with emotion. "What about me? I'm still fighting, and I'm tired of it. I'm tired of everything, period."

"What does that mean?"

"The lies. The betrayals. The manipulations. I worked so hard to get here, but I can't be just a college student. I can't just have a panic attack over a final exam like every other college student. Instead I have to worry about a freaking coup."

"You're so strong. So brave. You shouldn't have to be, but you are."

I shake my head, dislodging his hand, breaking the connection between us. "I can't stay here, not anymore. Not after everything that's happened. And besides, the scholarship money is gone. There's nothing left for me here."

"Then I'll pay your way."

"Don't."

"Why the hell wouldn't I?"

"Don't say it. Don't think it. It's not happening."

He takes a step closer, his eyes never leaving mine. "I'll pay for your education. You don't have to leave Tanglewood. You can stay, you can study, you can graduate."

I shake my head. "No."

His eyes flash, a storm brewing in their depths. "Why the hell not?"

"Because I'm not going to take your money, that's why. We're sleeping together. We're lovers. Or at least, we *were* lovers. So I can't take your money."

"Why was it okay for me to pay you when we were at the hotel, but not here?"

"Because it was different then," I say, my voice steadier than I feel. "It was a temporary solution. And you were a stranger."

"Bullshit. You needed help, and I provided it. Let me do that again."

I take a deep breath, trying to calm the storm of emotions raging within me. "It's not the same. That was a onetime thing. This is my education. An entire semester of tuition at one of the most expensive schools, an entire semester of room and board at outrageous prices, especially considering the state of the meatloaf. I can't accept that from you."

He takes another step closer, his voice dropping to a low, intense murmur. "Why not? Do you think I would make you pay me back?"

"Partly," I admit, my voice barely above a whisper, though it wouldn't be in money or interest. It wouldn't even be in sexual favors. I would have to pay him with loyalty. With devotion. And I've seen how those things can wrap around my wrists tighter than the ropes in the cathedral. They almost trapped me in Port Lavaca. "I don't want to owe you anything. I don't want to be…beholden to you."

He reaches out, his hand cupping my chin, forcing me to meet his gaze. "It would be a gift, with no strings attached."

I shake my head, dislodging his hand, breaking the connection between us. "There are always strings," I say, my voice thick with resignation. "Nothing in life is free. Everything has a cost, a price to pay. And I can't… I won't pay that price."

He stares at me, his eyes searching, probing. "What are you so afraid of?"

"Nothing."

"What are you running from?"

"Why are you chasing me?"

He reaches out, his hand cupping my cheek, his thumb brushing away a tear I hadn't even realized had fallen. His touch is gentle, tender, a stark contrast to the storm of emotions raging in his eyes. "You don't have to do this alone," he says, his voice intent.

"It's the only way I know how."

His eyes darken, a storm brewing in their depths as he takes a step closer. "Fine," he says, his voice a low growl. "Then get on the bed."

Shock courses through me. "What are you doing?"

"If you want to get paid for sex, then I'll pay you for sex."

Anger surges within me, hot and fierce, at his words, at his presumption. "How dare you," I say, my voice shaking with emotion. Or arousal. Maybe both.

"Lie down. Spread your legs. Prepare to get worked over, because if I'm going to pay for a semester of tuition at an expensive college, along with room and board—" He glances around the small room, clearly unimpressed. When he sees the yellow stain shaped like a tree, he shakes his head. "Then you're going to have to earn it."

His hands grip my shoulders, and he gently, gently, gently pushes me back onto the bed. I can stop him. I'm almost sure that I could, but I don't get to find out.

Because I let him tip me over.

My gasp is real, not out of shock or even true anger.

It's the arousal that pulses through me at the show of control.

He looks down on me, like a god surveying a sacrifice. "If you're so insistent on paying your own way, on not accepting my help, then fine. I'll pay you for the one thing I know you can give me. The one thing I know we both want."

I struggle beneath him, trying to push him away, but he's too strong, too solid. And I don't really want to win. "Get off me."

He ignores my protests, his hands gripping my wrists, pinning them above my head. I buck against him, trying to dislodge him, but he doesn't budge, his body a solid weight on top of mine. "Stop fighting me," he says, his voice a low murmur, his breath hot against my ear.

"I won't have sex with you. Not here."

"You want it here more than anywhere else. Where you're just poor little Ms. Hill, and I'm Professor Stratford. That's how you want it."

I shake my head, denying his words, denying the truth in them. "No," I say, my voice barely above a whisper. "I don't."

He ignores my protests, his mouth capturing mine in a fierce, demanding kiss. I struggle against him, trying to turn my head away, but he's relentless, his tongue invading my mouth, his teeth nipping at my lips.

I can taste the desperation in his kiss, the hunger, the need. And despite myself, despite my anger, my body responds, heat pooling in my core, my breath coming in ragged pants.

He breaks the kiss, his mouth trailing down my neck, his teeth grazing the sensitive skin. I shiver, a gasp escaping my lips, my body betraying me, responding to his touch despite my mind's protests. "William," I say, my voice a plea, a desperate cry. "Please. I can't."

He ignores my pleas, his hands rough and demanding as they roam over my body, squeezing, caressing, possessing. I struggle against him, but my struggles are weak, my body melting beneath his touch, my mind clouded with desire and need. He grips the hem of my shirt, pulling it up and over my head, baring my skin to his hungry gaze. His eyes darken, a growl rumbling in his chest as he takes in the sight of me, half-naked and vulnerable beneath him.

"Professor," I moan.

He silences me with another fierce kiss, his body pressing against mine, his hardness grinding against my core. I gasp, my body arching against him, my mind a whirl of confusion and desire and need.

He breaks the kiss, his mouth trailing down my body, his tongue licking, his teeth nipping, his hands rough and demanding. I'm lost in a sea of sensation, my body responding to his touch, my mind clouded with desire. I know I should stop him, should push him away, but I can't. My body betrays me, my need for him overwhelming my senses.

He grips the waistband of my pants, tugging them down, baring me to his hungry gaze. I shiver, a gasp escaping my lips as he trails his fingers up my inner thigh, his touch light, teasing, a stark contrast to the rough demand of his earlier touch. I'm trembling, my body aching with need, my mind a whirl of confusion and desire.

"Spread your legs," he says again, his voice a low growl.

And despite myself, despite my mind's protests, I obey.

My legs fall open, baring myself to him completely.

CHAPTER NINETEEN

Quiet Corner

I WAKE UP to the soft glow of morning light filtering through the thin curtains of my dorm room. My body aches in a delicious way, a reminder of the night spent with William.

His scent, a mix of musk and the faint hint of old books, lingers on the pillow beneath my cheek. I can feel the steady rise and fall of his chest against my back, his arm draped possessively around my waist.

It's a startling sensation, having him here in the morning, in my dorm room. A thrill courses through me, a dangerous dance with the possibility of being caught. The Shakespeare Society is no more, their tendrils of power snipped. Maybe, just maybe, we're safe.

I stretch languidly, my muscles protesting slightly. The soreness between my thighs sends a shiver down my spine, my body still humming from his touch.

I can't help but smile, a secret, satisfied curve of my lips.

But as consciousness fully descends, so do my worries.

The societal debris may have been cleared, but the path forward isn't suddenly smooth. My tuition remains a looming shadow, a problem I can't solve by simply closing my eyes and wishing it away.

The sex we had was rough. And fun.

But I won't use it to pay for tuition.

I turn to face him, his features soft in sleep.

The usual stern lines of his face are smoothed out, making him look younger, almost boyish. My heart flutters, a warm sensation spreading through me. I could get used to this, I think, then swiftly banish the thought. No, I can't depend on him, on anyone. I need to figure this out on my own.

His eyes flutter open, catching me in his gaze. A slow smile spreads across his face, and he pulls me closer, his voice a low rumble. "Morning."

I hesitate, then smile back. "Morning."

His hand trails down my side, igniting sparks in its wake. I'm suddenly very aware of my body, of his, of the heat building between us. I lose myself in his touch, his kiss. Right now, in his arms, is the only certainty I have. And I cling to it, desperate and hungry, as the world outside looms, waiting.

The warmth of his body seeps into mine, his hand tracing patterns on my skin. I can feel the hard length of him pressed against my thigh, a silent promise. His eyes, those intense, dark eyes, hold me captive.

There's no escape, not that I want one. Not really.

"What are you thinking about?" His voice is a low rumble, vibrating through me.

I hesitate, then admit, "Everything. Nothing."

He raises an eyebrow, his thumb circling my nipple, drawing out a gasp. "That's not an answer."

I arch into his touch, my body already alight. "I'm thinking about how much I want you. About how wrong this is, but how right it feels."

A slow smile spreads across his face. He leans in, his breath hot on my ear. "I like it when you're honest."

His hand trails down, over my stomach, my hips, until he's cupping me. I'm already wet, my body ready for him. He groans, his fingers slipping inside me. "You're always so ready for me."

I can't respond, can't do anything but feel. His fingers move expertly, stroking, teasing. My hips buck against his hand, chasing the sensation. He watches me, his eyes never leaving mine. It's intense, intimate. I'm laid bare, not just physically, but emotionally. He sees me, all of me, and he wants me.

He shifts, his body covering mine. His cock presses against my entrance, a tantalizing promise. But he doesn't push in, not yet. He holds himself there, his muscles trembling with restraint. "Tell me you want me," he demands.

I look into his eyes, seeing the raw need reflected there. It's a heady feeling, knowing I have this power over him. "I want you," I whisper.

With a groan, he pushes into me. My body stretches to accommodate him, that delicious burn making me gasp. He starts to move, slow at first, then faster, harder. Each thrust hits a spot deep inside me, sending waves of pleasure coursing through me.

I cling to him, my nails digging into his back. He growls, his pace quickening. The room fills with the sound of our bodies coming together, the scent of sex and sweat. It's primal, raw. It's us.

His hand slips between us, his fingers finding

my clit. He rubs in time with his thrusts, pushing me higher, closer to the edge. I can feel it building, that intense pressure. I'm so close, so very close.

"Come for me, brave heart. Let me feel your sweet little pussy grip my cock."

His words push me over the edge. I cry out, my body convulsing around him. He groans, his hips jerking as he finds his own release. We ride out the waves together, our bodies slick with sweat, our breaths ragged.

In the aftermath, he rolls off me, pulling me into his arms. I can feel his heart pounding, echoing my own. I look up at him, this man who has become my world. His eyes are closed, his face relaxed. He looks almost peaceful.

But as I lie here, wrapped in his arms, I can't help but wonder what happens next. Where do we go from here? The future is uncertain, a vast unknown. But for now, in this moment, I'm exactly where I want to be.

I trace the lines of his face, my fingers lingering on his lips. His eyes flutter open, catching me in his gaze. He smiles, that slow, sexy smile that never fails to make my heart race.

"Good morning," he murmurs, his voice a low rumble.

I can't help but smile back. "Good morning indeed."

He shifts, propping himself up on one elbow to look down at me. His fingers trail lightly over my shoulder, down my arm, leaving goose bumps in their wake. "There's something I need to tell you."

"Oh?"

"Thank you. For saving Brandon."

"Oh."

"The plan was already in motion. I didn't know you'd be taken. I didn't—"

"Don't. Don't blame yourself for what they did. And don't keep trying to protect me. You can't keep secrets from me if you trust me."

He shakes his head, because he still clearly *doesn't* trust me, even though I know he wouldn't agree with that. "I never stopped thinking about you. Even when I was supposed to stay away, I couldn't. You were always on my mind."

"I missed you, too. When I thought you were *dead*."

"You're not just a student to me, brave heart. You never were."

"Then why didn't you trust me?"

He sighs, his expression turning serious. "This again."

"Yes," I say, frustrated. "This again. This forever."

His answer is an angry, dominating kiss, his body pressing against mine. I can feel his desire, hard and insistent against my thigh. It's offensive for him to think that he can answer a serious question with sex.

At least, it's offensive in theory.

In reality my body responds, heat pooling between my legs.

His hands roam over my body, touching, teasing. I gasp as he finds a particularly sensitive spot, my hips bucking against him. He chuckles, a low, sexy sound that sends shivers down my spine.

"You like that, brave heart?" he murmurs, his lips trailing down my neck.

I can only nod, my breath coming in short gasps. He knows my body so well, knows exactly what I need, what I want. And I want him. All of him.

His mouth finds my breast, his tongue circling my nipple. I arch into him, a moan escaping my lips. He sucks, bites, driving me wild with desire. I can feel the pressure building, the need for release growing stronger with each touch, each kiss.

But just as I'm about to tumble over the edge,

he pulls back, a wicked grin on his face. I groan in frustration, but he just laughs, his eyes dark with desire.

"Patience," he says. "We have all the time in the world."

Except he's wrong.

We're running out of time.

He starts all over again, his touch lighter this time, teasing, tantalizing. I squirm beneath him, my body aching for more. I beg for him to take me. But he takes his time, drawing out the pleasure, driving me wild with need.

Finally, he slides into me.

I gasp. I'm completely filled by him.

He starts to move, slow at first, then faster, harder. Each thrust hits a spot deep inside me, sending waves of pleasure coursing through me.

His hand slips between us, his fingers finding my clit. He rubs in time with his thrusts, pushing me higher, closer to the edge. I can feel it building, that intense pressure.

I'm so close, so very close.

"Come for me," he orders, his voice rough.

His words push me over the edge.

The pinch of pain on my clit makes it explosive.

I cry out, my body convulsing around him.

He groans, his hips jerking as he finds his own release, finding solace in my body, ignoring my needs and my fears, wanting to pleasure me into obedience.

The faintest scuff outside the door.

I barely have time to drag the sheets over us as Daisy walks in.

Her blue eyes widen. "Wow."

"Christ," William mutters, shielding me with his body.

It's a sweet, chivalrous gesture, even though Daisy and I have been roommates for over three years. She's already seen me naked. She's never seen *him* naked. Her blue eyes take in his muscular body with clear appreciation.

"Daisy," I say, my face warm. I'm not sure whether I'm more scandalized by her obvious appraisal or by the fact that I feel…jealousy. How mundane of me.

"I would tell you two to get a room, but it's clear you already did." Her eyes dance with amusement. "Though next time leave a sock on the door. I think that's how roommates do it when one of them's having sex."

"There's not going to be a next time."

The door closes behind her.

I cover my face. "Oh my god."

William strokes my hair, his voice rough with sleep and pleasure, a tinge of wry amusement in his voice. "You didn't already have a signal for this?"

"Of course not."

"Then that means you never brought a boy back."

The satisfaction in his voice makes my eyes narrow. "Get out."

"Fine. I really do have to go. There's all kinds of red tape that needs to be handled, both for the university and for the police. But don't think we're done here. You and I are going to come to an understanding on this. You're not dropping out. Period."

CHAPTER TWENTY

Merit Alone

"OKAY," DAISY SAYS. "Girl time."

"What's girl time?" I ask, eyeing her nervously. Neither of us is the type to spend time shopping or getting manicures. We don't have the money for such things, which is partly why we don't do those things.

"We could build compression engines using paper clips?"

That's the other reason why we don't do those things. I would rather read an old manuscript. And she would rather engineer something. "Pass."

"Fine. *Fine.* We'll analyze a sordid drama with danger and desire worthy of a Victorian-era stage."

"Shakespeare was Elizabethan."

"Whatever."

She's talking about William, of course. And me. "What is there to say?"

"You could tell me how good the sex is."

"TMI."

"I'm the receiver," she says. "I get to decide if something is *too much information*, and it's decidedly not."

The campus is still in complete disarray, as more and more details spill out.

Everyone has a story about Thorne now, about how she was rude to someone on the stairs, about how she once picked a flower from the biology department's botanical center, even though you're not allowed to. Even though what she did was truly awful, the pile-on is embarrassing. Next we're going to hear that she kicked puppies for fun.

Everyone wants to be involved in the story, so they have something to add even if they only saw her in passing one day in the entire semester.

"I don't know what's going to happen with us," I confess, hugging a pillow to my chest. The dorm room feels small, intimate, a safe space to voice my doubts. "The sex is…well, you know."

"I can guess, but I'd love details," she drawls.

I ignore this. "I think he cares about me. I mean, really cares. But what kind of future can we have? He's so much older, and I'm…me. Broke, confused, still in college."

"And the problem is?"

"The problem is, it would be uneven. He has all the power. He wants to pay for my tuition, for God's sake."

She laughs. "And that's a bad thing because…?"

"Because I don't want it to be uneven between us."

"I've seen you two together. You challenge him. You make him think. And he does the same for you. You're both crazy about Shakespeare, about literature. I've never seen two people more evenly matched."

"I challenge him to stay alive."

She raises an eyebrow, not taking the bait. "If he's offering to help with tuition, it's because he cares. It's not about power or control. It's about him wanting to support you, to help you reach your goals."

I sigh, looking down at the pillow in my lap. "I just don't know if it's enough. If we're enough."

"*You* are enough, Anne. That's the part you can't accept. You always treated the scholarship as some kind of clerical error, as if you could accept it but you never believed you deserved it. Now that you're faced with finding another way, with accepting help from someone who loves you, it's harder. But it's real."

A lump forms in my throat. "You're right."

"Of course I am," she says with casual aplomb. "You have to end up together. After all, who else will put up with either of you. I bet you guys even recite Shakespeare during sex."

My cheeks flush with heat, remembering.

"Oh my God, it's true!"

I can't help but laugh even as my cheeks burn, the tension in the room breaking. Maybe she's right. Maybe William and I are more evenly matched than I thought. Maybe, just maybe, we have a chance at a future together. But even as I laugh, a small voice in the back of my mind whispers, *What if it's not enough?*

I pace the small length of the dorm room, my fingers tracing the chipped paint on the walls. Daisy watches me from her bed, her legs crossed, her hands folded in her lap. She's unperturbable. I could tell her anything.

"He's so much older than me," I say, turning to face her. "Like, almost twenty years older. Isn't that weird?"

Daisy tilts her head, considering. "Age is just a number."

"So is the golden ratio."

She gasps, only half kidding. "Take that back."

"What will people think?" I ask, chewing on my lower lip.

Daisy rolls her eyes. "Who cares what people think?"

I sigh, running a hand through my hair. "I don't know. I just…I never expected this. I never expected him. And I definitely never expected him to be the father of my ex-boyfriend."

"Let me get this straight. He's good enough for a tryst, but not good enough to marry? You're going to make him feel cheap."

I stick my tongue out at her. "God, it's like a soap opera."

"It's like Shakespeare," she says with a cheeky grin. "*The son scorned, the father adored, the romance hath been thus foresworn.*"

"Okay, that's annoyingly good."

Daisy laughs, a full-throated sound that fills the room. "If the whole engineering thing doesn't work out, I'm going to become the modern-day Bard."

I flop down on my bed, staring up at the yellow stain on the ceiling. "Maybe. But it's not just about me. It's about William too. His reputation, his career. What people will think of him for being with a student."

"Or it could make him happier than he's ever been," Daisy counters. "You can't live your life worried about what might happen. You have to take risks, take chances. Otherwise, you'll never know what could have been."

I turn my head to look at her. "When did you get so wise?"

"I've always been wise. You're just finally listening."

I grin, some of the tension easing in my chest. "I don't want to be a dirty little secret. I don't want to be something he's ashamed of."

"Then don't be," she says, her voice firm. "You're worth more than that. The scariest part might be that he knows that, too."

I take a deep breath, letting her words sink in. She's right. I can't live my life in the shadows, always worried about what people might think. I have to take a chance, take a risk. I have to fight for what I want.

And what I want is William.

However, I also want an academic career, one that isn't tainted. Gossip about my sex life is one thing. Rumors about my ethics are another.

"What about the essay, the claims that he wrote it for me? Even with Thorne discredited, people will still talk."

Her blue eyes flash with fierce loyalty. "Fuck them."

"The life of an academic isn't a solitary one. You have to get your papers accepted by peers. You have to get invited to speak at events. This isn't about vanity. It's about my entire career. Or lack of one."

"Shit," she says with a sigh. "Engineering isn't the same. Like yeah, there's an academic community, but there are also practical uses. There's an entire world out there to make your mark—and make money."

"There are no corporations dedicated to decoding Shakespearean symbolism or identifying a particular source in a sonnet. Unfortunately. Only the academics who will assume I'm only with him for what he can do for my career. That I'm so ambitious I would sleep with him to get him to write stuff for me."

"I know Thorne was an asshole, but don't let her give ambition a bad name. Ambition is just wanting to try things, wanting them to work out. It's wrong for society to make it such a bad word for women when men are praised for the same thing."

"You're right." I shake my head, as if to clear

it. "She was cruel and dishonest. That's different."

Daisy leans forward, her voice firm. "You're not with William for what he can do for you. You're with him because you love him, because he challenges you, because he makes you a better version of yourself."

"You're right. I know you're right. But it's still scary." I swallow around a lump in my throat, my voice dropping to a whisper. "I'm not as strong as you are."

"Bullshit."

"It's true."

A snort that's somehow feminine when she does it. "You stood up to your parents. You fought for your education. You didn't let them hold you back, and you can't let anyone hold you back now."

"I'm tired."

Her expression softens. "I know, sweetheart."

"But I'm here for the work. If they don't accept my papers or ask me to talk, I can still study. And if they won't pay me, I can wait tables at diners in between my research. I'll do what it takes."

Her expression softens. "Of course you will."

A renewed sense of determination surges through me. I can't let the whispers and judgments of others hold me back. I can't let them define me.

I have to define myself.

I take a deep breath, steeling myself for what I'm about to say. Daisy watches me, her blue eyes curious and concerned. She knows I've been wrestling with this, knows how torn I've been.

"I'm going to be with William," I say, my voice steady. "Anything else would be cowardly. And not deserving of a Shakespearean scholar. If he taught us anything, it's to experience love no matter the consequences. Because I do love him."

Daisy claps. "Finally! It's about time you admitted it."

"But there's one thing I won't do."

"Uh-oh."

"I won't take his money. No, don't bother arguing with me. I can't. I won't let money poison what we have, like it did with my parents. I won't let it turn us into something ugly, something toxic."

"It doesn't have to be like that."

Except I have a lifetime of conditioning showing me that it does. I saw how money poisoned my parents' lives, their desperate quest for more and more money, their deep-set co-dependence, the way neither can live apart even though they're miserable. I won't let that happen to me, not even for William.

"We can be together without him paying for my tuition."

Daisy tugs on a strand of her blonde hair. "There's nothing wrong with help. You would want to help him if the situations were reversed."

"As if he would let me."

"No, you're right. Men get stubborn about stuff like that."

"And if men are allowed to be stubborn, then so are women."

"You're right. Unfortunately."

"I can't let him buy me, buy my time, my devotion. I can't let him expect things from me, even if he doesn't mean to. I won't be owned, not even by William."

If I take his money, he will expect things from me. He won't do it on purpose, but he will. Everyone does. When they pay for something, for someone, when they buy someone, they expect their time, their devotion. They expect to be able to hurt them, maybe even in small ways, and I can't go there.

"I love him, but I have to protect myself too. I have to make sure that what we have is real, that it's not just about power or control. I have to keep my identity."

Daisy's expression is sober. "I understand."

Of course she does. She knows a lot about power and control.

The version she came from was more rustic than even my small-town environment, but the result is the same. Women, trapped and hurt and afraid. Part of me knows that William wouldn't do that, but this fear was formed a long time ago. I learned it when I was a child, when I was a baby. I probably understood it in the womb, some ancient heartbeat that warned me about the world I would enter.

"Maybe I should just try to get over it."

"Absolutely not."

"I thought you'd want me to."

"I want you to graduate, yeah, but you've done the impossible, getting to Tanglewood University, getting such good grades, being so close to the finish line despite the odds that were stacked against you. How many people that you went to high school with did this?"

Almost no one.

It's part of why I found my refuge in books. I had nothing in common with the people there. Some of the girls were already getting pregnant. They were pairing up, preparing for a life spent as factory workers, as diner waitresses. There's nothing shameful about those professions, but I always knew that I was meant to do *this*.

Her voice softens. "You didn't come this far to only come this far."

"It's a rock and a hard place. The rock is leaving Tanglewood, even temporarily, which I have to do without the scholarship money. The hard place is…"

"The hard place is William Stratford's anatomy, I'm guessing."

"Well…yes. It's also his money."

"Do I think you should get over it? You set the standards for your life for a reason. And they worked. They'll keep working. That means not letting a fuckboy like Brandon derail you, even when he was cheating on you."

Holy shit. "I just realized that Carlisle outed him, too."

At Daisy's confusion, I explain how she created Tanglewood Tea.

That means she's the one who posted a photo of Brandon making out with a girl in Ibiza. That hurt, but it also helped. Better to know the truth, even if it's painful. I've only ever wanted knowledge. I always knew it was the antidote to fear.

Daisy whistles. "I mean, damn. I know we're pissed at her, but that's kind of impressive. Especially considering she'd be super conspicuous wherever she goes."

"She moved out of her dorm room." A knot forms in my throat. I'm worried for her. Regardless of my anger. Escaping is a solo activity. I knew that early on. I knew that if I tried to bring the world with me, I'd have no chance. But leaving people I love behind doesn't feel right, either. "I hope she's okay."

"She probably just moved into an even nicer one, like they tore down the walls of the top floor to create a penthouse dorm room. The university has ambition, too. It loves having the hottest child actress and pop star as a student."

Applications to the music department went up when she enrolled. The music department got a new building, under construction, courtesy of uber rich alumni—whose daughter wanted to meet Carlisle Storm. She played her part, attending the private dinner, even singing for the private audience.

In fact, I read about that on Tanglewood Tea.

Performing Monkey Does Tricks for Coins, the caption had said.

Carlisle wrote that about herself. Bile rises in

my throat. I remember it specifically, because I remember thinking how much it must hurt her to read it. It probably did hurt her. To write it. To know it. Maybe I can understand the perverse way it helped to be the person who told everyone, rather than to let it come out on its own. Or to keep it inside.

The university does love having her as a student.

I think they also resent her.

We all want to succeed on merit alone. Me. Daisy.

The university.

But even they know it's never enough.

CHAPTER TWENTY-ONE
Cliff's Notes

'M WALKING BACK from the library late at night, my arms laden with books. The campus is quiet, the usual hum of students absent, thanks to the late hour. I'm lost in thought, the events of the past few weeks playing on a loop in my mind.

I don't notice the black car pulling up beside me until it's too late.

The door swings open, a gloved hand reaching out and grabbing my arm. I'm pulled off-balance, books scattering across the pavement. I open my mouth to scream, but a hand clamps down, muffling the sound. I'm shoved into the car, the door slamming shut behind me. The car speeds off, leaving my books strewn across the sidewalk.

I struggle, kicking and biting, but my captor is strong.

He pins me down, his face coming into view. Luca Andini. His eyes are wild, desperate. I stop struggling, shock coursing through me.

"What the hell are you doing?" I demand, my voice shaking.

Luca's laugh is harsh, bitter. "I'm taking matters into my own hands."

The car speeds through the night, leaving the campus behind. I look out the window, trying to memorize the route, but the streets are a blur. We pull up to the large old manor house, the same one we were in where the blasphemous ceremony took place.

Iron gates slam shut behind us.

Luca drags me out of the car, his grip bruising. I look around, taking in the dimly lit space. It's filled with crates and boxes, a maze of shadows. I try to pull away, but Luca's grip tightens.

"Let me go," I say, my voice steady despite the fear coursing through me.

Luca shakes his head, a cruel smile playing on his lips. "I can't do that, Ms. Hill. You're my insurance policy."

"Insurance policy?" I echo, confusion warring with fear.

Luca nods, pulling me toward a chair in the center of the room. He forces me to sit, his hands rough as he ties my wrists behind my back. "Yes, you see, I'm in a bit of a predicament. Thanks to that meddling friend of yours and her little blog, I've lost everything. My position, my power, my money."

"You mean the money you stole," I say, anger rising.

Luca's eyes flash, but he doesn't deny it. "Yes, well, it was mine to take. And now, thanks to you and your friends, I'm a wanted man. I can't leave the country; I can't access my accounts. I'm trapped."

"So, what, you're going to hold me hostage until what? They give you a plane and a pile of cash?" I scoff, even as fear snakes up my spine.

Luca leans in, his face inches from mine. His eyes are bloodshot, his breath reeking of desperation. "I'm a cornered wolf, Ms. Hill. And cornered wolves are dangerous. I have nothing left to lose, and that makes me very, very unstable."

His words send a chill down my spine. I'm in deep trouble. I need to find a way out, and fast. But for now, I'm at Luca's mercy, trapped in this basement with a desperate, dangerous man. I take a deep breath, trying to steady my nerves. I need to keep my wits about me if I'm going to survive this.

"You think this is going to work?" I say, my

voice steady despite the fear coursing through me. "You think holding me hostage is going to get you what you want?"

He paces. "It's the only chance I have left."

"And what happens when they catch you?"

His eyes flash, a muscle in his jaw twitching. "I have a plan."

"A plan?" I scoff. "Like the plan you had to steal from the scholarship fund? Like the plan you had to take over the liberal arts department? Look how well those turned out."

His eyes are cold, calculating. "You think you're clever, don't you? You think you have it all figured out. But you don't know anything. You don't know the power I hold, the connections I have."

"Power?" I laugh, a harsh, bitter sound. "What power do you have left, Luca? You're a disgraced professor on the run. You have nothing left."

"I have you, Ms. Hill. And that's enough."

"Enough for what?" It's not a great idea to taunt a man holding a gun, but I'm through being meek for him. And for the Society. I'm a cornered wolf, too. I've already lost everything that mattered to me. "Enough to get you killed? Because that's what's going to happen. You think you're the first desperate man to take a hostage? You think this is going to end well for you?"

His voice drops to a low growl. "It will if you cooperate."

"Cooperate?" I echo. "You think I'm going to help you?"

A cold, cruel smile. "I think you're going to do exactly what I say, Ms. Hill. Because if you don't, people are going to get hurt. And I don't think you want that on your conscience."

I stare at him, my heart pounding in my chest. "Fuck you."

He laughs. "This is power. Didn't you read *Macbeth*?"

"Yes, and I read about his head on a pike. Or didn't you read your copy of Cliff's Notes to the end?"

He narrows his eyes at me, not liking the insult. Good.

"You're going to regret that," he says, his voice low, dangerous. "You're going to regret ever crossing me." His eyes gleam with a sickening lust as he reaches out, his hand tracing the line of my jaw.

I flinch away, but he grips my chin, forcing me to look at him.

"You know, I've always wondered what Stratford saw in you," he muses, his thumb brushing over my bottom lip. "Now I think I understand."

I gather every ounce of courage and saliva in my mouth and spit, hitting him square in the face. His expression darkens, and before I can brace myself, his hand cracks across my cheek.

Pain explodes in my face, stars dancing in my vision.

"You little bitch," he growls, wiping his face with the back of his hand.

Suddenly, the door to the basement creaks open, and Matteo steps in. My heart leaps at the sight of him, hope surging. He's always been a jerk, but surely he won't stand for this.

Luca turns to him, a scowl on his face. "What are you doing here?"

Matteo avoids my gaze, his expression unreadable. "You left your phone in the car. I thought you might need it."

Luca snatches the phone from Matteo's hand, his eyes narrowing. "You shouldn't be down here."

Matteo's gaze flickers to me, then away. "People will notice if she's gone."

"Let them wonder."

A tense nod. Matteo knows this is wrong. I can see it in his eyes. But he says nothing, does nothing. My spirits sink as I realize he's not here to help me.

Luca turns back to me. "I have some business to attend to. But don't worry, I'll be back soon. And then we can continue where we left off."

CHAPTER TWENTY-TWO

Not Very Shakespearean

MATTEO CARRIES A tray with a bottle of water and what appears to be a sandwich wrapped in plastic. It looks like the kind you get in the stop-and-go delis on campus, alongside string cheese, bottled water, and number two pencils. We're far away from campus now, but the tendrils of the school wraps around us—for good or for evil.

His footsteps echoing in the cavernous space. This is the same place where his father threatened to have sex with me as part of some society ritual. The same place where William saved me…by doing it himself. It was a problematic method of protection but one that I infinitely preferred. Matteo's hair is disheveled, not in the fashionable, debonair way it usually is. It looks messy, and faintly oily, as if he hasn't showered in days. There are dark circles under his eyes. This is a far cry from the literary king of campus.

His eyes meet mine, and for a moment, he hesitates, his gaze flickering over my face. I'm sure I look even worse, my cheek still stinging from Luca's slap, my eyes puffy from dry tears. I lift my chin, refusing to show him how scared I actually am.

Matteo walks over, setting the tray down on the rickety table beside me. He doesn't say a word, just pushes the bottle of water toward me. I stare at it, then at him, suspicion coiling in my gut. I want it, but my hands are tied—literally.

Does he want me to beg? I wish I could be sure I wouldn't.

"What are you doing?" My voice comes out rusty.

"You need to eat. And drink."

"You're suddenly concerned about my well-being? Why is that hard to believe?"

Matteo's jaw tightens. "Just…take it, okay?"

A lump forms in my throat, tears pricking at the back of my eyes. I blink them away, opening my lips. Matteo fumbles with the cap. His hands tremble slightly as he tips the plastic bottle to my lips. Cool liquid soothes my parched throat.

I can't help but close my eyes in relief.

Matteo watches me, his eyes unreadable. "You

need your strength."

"For what? So your dad can rape me?"

He flinches. "Don't talk like that."

"You have to let me go. This is kidnapping. It's crazy."

"It's already done."

"So undo it."

His eyes flick away from mine. "I'm in too deep."

"Too deep?" I echo, disbelief coloring my voice. "You're not a criminal. You're a student, a *scholar*, a brilliant one. You have your whole life ahead of you. Don't throw it away for…for this."

"You don't understand. My father…he's not a man you say *no* to."

I did, though that didn't seem to help. "So, what?" I say, my voice rising. "You're just going to do whatever he says? Kidnap innocent people? Hurt them?"

His gaze flicks to my cheek. "I never wanted you to get hurt."

"Then help me," I say, my voice filled with urgency. "Let me go. Please."

"I can't. I wish I could, but… I can't."

Frustration and anger bubble inside me. "That's an excuse. Too many people in the world have said they had no choice. It's self-interest and ambition disguised as fear."

His head snaps up, his eyes flashing. "You think I'm ambitious? You're the one who wanted the fucking Tempest Prize so badly. I told you to leave it alone."

"I'm the one who *won* it. You're the one who *stole* it. That's the difference."

"I didn't want them to cheat."

"It happened anyway."

"Which is just fucking proof that I have no control over the situation."

He's not going to help me. I lean back, the cold metal of the chair pressing into my spine, a sigh escaping my lips, ignoring him as he goes to stand by the door.

I'm unimpressed by this so-called lack of choice.

It's a stark contrast to me. To Daisy. To all the scholarship students in Hathaway who saw their futures go up in smoke, even though the Andinis were already wealthy.

We fought against our circumstances, against the hands we were dealt. Matteo thinks he has no choice, but that's an illusion. One that conveniently serves him. There's always a choice. It might not be easy. It might not even be safe, but it's there.

Privilege isn't just about having more clothes and a nice car.

It's about believing that you can be a victim of your circumstances, even as you accept a prize you don't deserve and obey your criminal father. It's about pretending you don't have control even as you steal and lie and hurt people around you.

The cavernous basement looks even larger without the crowd of hooded society members. I need to find a way out, a weapon, anything. My eyes land on a pile of old crates in the corner, dusty and forgotten. I doubt there's anything useful, but I have to check.

I stand up, my chair scraping against the concrete floor.

Matteo's head snaps up, his eyes narrowing. "What are you doing?"

"I need to pee," I say, my voice steady despite the pounding of my heart.

Matteo hesitates. "Fine. But make it quick."

He stands up, gesturing for me to follow him. I do, my heart pounding in my chest. He leads me to a small, grimy bathroom, the door creaking as he opens it. My hands are still tied in front of me. He makes no move to untie them, so I guess I have to go like this.

"I'll be right outside," he says, his voice a

warning.

Inside, the faucet sputters to life. I splash some water on my face, my reflection staring back at me in the cracked mirror.

The young woman looks battered.

And determined.

She looks like a fighter.

Which is nice. I wish the reflection would share some bravery with me.

I flush the toilet, the sound echoing in the small space. I take a deep breath, then another. I step out of the bathroom, my heart pounding in my chest. Matteo leans against the wall, his arms crossed over his chest.

He straightens up as I approach, his eyes narrowing.

"Can I have some more water?" I ask, my voice soft, innocent. I need to keep him distracted, need him to think I'm compliant, cooperative. "Please."

He sighs. "I'll be right back."

I watch him go, my heart in my throat. This is it. This is my chance.

When he's gone, I rush back to the pile of crates. They're made of wood. Nailed shut.

Damn it.

What's inside?

Anything useful like a weapon? Or maybe just a bunch of cotton fluff that wouldn't help? I can't find out. Except that when I nudge one, it's clearly heavy. Well. This will have to do. It's a large, blunt object.

Not very elegant.

Not very Shakespearean.

Good thing I don't need Shakespeare to survive.

I position myself behind a crate, heart pounding like a drum in my chest. I can hear footsteps approaching. There's only one shot. He won't trust me again. The door creaks open, and Matteo steps in. I watch him from behind as he scans the room.

"Anne?" he calls out, his voice echoing in the vast space.

He takes one step forward, then another. He's wary. That's why he turns, spinning—too late. I slam the crate into his shoulders.

It hits him with a sickening crack.

He crumples to the ground.

And groans.

Not dead, at least. Which is nice. I probably shouldn't care about that, but I'd rather not become a murderer tonight. Then I'm up and running up the stairs.

I need to get out of here, need to get back to campus.

I reach the door, my heart pounding in my chest. I'm so close, so close to freedom. I can taste it, can feel it. I need to make it out of this basement, out of this house. How far is this place from campus? Even farther than the woods, I think. And my hands are still tied. Maybe I can break through the rope with something I find in the woods.

I'm thinking too far in the future.

The door bursts open.

Luca stands at the top of the stairs. He surveys Matteo's splayed body, the cracked crate with a sneer. "You little bitch," he says, his voice a low, dangerous rumble. "You think you can outsmart me?"

I stare at him, my heart in my throat.

Yes, I thought I could. But clearly I was wrong.

And that might be the death of me.

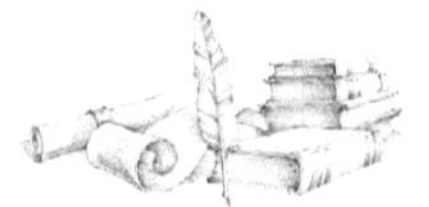

CHAPTER TWENTY-THREE

Dramatic Freaking Duel

LUCA HAS ME pinned to the ground. The weight of him makes me sick. It's a parody of what I shared with William. He tries to kiss me, his lips wet. It's more blasphemous than having sex in the tower of a cathedral.

No. This isn't happening.

I slam my head into his, leaving me stunned—and drawing blood. A drop of red mars his lips. He snarls, looking like a wild animal. Ambition without any trace of humanity. I fight him, using my bound fists to beat his shoulders. It doesn't seem to make much difference, but it doesn't stop me. I'd rather die fighting him than accept this.

A hard swipe across my cheek, the same place he hit me before.

Stars swirl in a miasma of pain.

When I manage to gain consciousness again,

he's already opened my jeans.

It excites him, I realize dimly, the way I fight him. He wants the drama of it, the same way he likes the pomp and circumstance of the secret society. It's a form of foreplay to him. He lacks soul, so regular pleasure would mean nothing.

I can't stop this.

I've failed.

My stomach turns over, but I don't even have enough inside to vomit on him.

I close my eyes, not wanting to see.

The heavy carved door slams open, the sound echoing like a gunshot. My heart pounds in surprise. And faint hope. Luca's face contorts with rage. And—sweet relief—he pushes off me to face the newcomers.

That's when I can finally see.

Standing in the doorway, like an avenging angel, is William.

Shock ripples through me, followed by a surge of relief so intense it makes my knees weak. William's eyes find mine, and the raw intensity in them steals my breath.

He's not the academic professor now.

He's a warrior, fierce and powerful, ready to fight the world for me.

His chest heaves, his muscles taut beneath his

shirt. His hair is disheveled. The stubble on his jaw accentuates the hard lines of his face. He's never looked more handsome, more commanding. More like home.

"Anne," he growls, his voice a low, dangerous rumble that sends shivers down my spine. It's a promise. The promise of safety. And retribution.

Behind him are two other men.

I recognize Professor Cormac Stratford. His rugged face is set in a scowl, his broad shoulders squared, ready for a fight. The other has the same powerful bone structure, although he's leaner, with darker hair, and even colder eyes. I'm assuming this is Asher, the third Stratford brother. Though it's hard to imagine this man as the author of moving symphonies. He looks like he could raze entire cities to the ground.

Luca takes a step back, his bravado faltering.

"Get them," he says to Matteo, who stands there, empty-handed, looking torn. There's obviously nothing he can do against such a wall of power. But he's already chosen his side, the losing one. This is what happens when you cheat. Once you realize you can take what you want without anyone stopping you, you want more. And there will always be one more thing you'll want, one more thing you don't deserve that will be your downfall.

I push myself to sitting, scooting away from the men.

They're outmatched. And they know it.

William takes a step forward, his eyes never leaving mine. The air crackles with tension, with the promise of violence. "Cover her," he says.

Cormac seems to know what it means. He steps in front of me, a human shield. Meanwhile, Asher circles Luca and Matteo, removing a retreat.

"You're outnumbered," William says. "Will you submit?"

Cormac stands with his fists at his sides, clearly ready to use them. Asher says nothing, his silence chilling. There's music even in his stillness.

"No," Luca says.

"Then we'll fight. You and me. One on one."

My eyes widen. "No."

Luca sneers. "A fair fight? You would lose."

William steps forward, his eyes meeting mine. The air crackles with tension, with the promise of violence. He's the calm before the storm, the eye of the hurricane. He's the general of the army, the one who will burn the world in retribution.

The one who will reclaim the throne…for me.

"Anne," he says, his voice a low, dangerous rumble. "Did he hurt you?"

"He—" My voice cracks. "He tried."

His expression firms. "I'll make him pay for that."

"Don't," I say, not wanting him to be hurt. They have the upper hand. They can call the cops. They can end this, where everyone walks away safe. And alive.

"We settle this like gentlemen." Luca smiles, as if he knows he's won. It chills me, that smile. "Have you been practicing with the sword? I doubt it. Not much time in between writing all those papers, giving all those lectures. Fucking all those students."

Dark eyes narrow. "Then we duel."

My heart lurches in my chest. "This is insane."

No one listens to me.

Asher digs into the crates, pulling out—props, basically. Stacks of hooded robes. Goblets. Eventually he finds long boxes that apparently hold swords. Good god. The secret society actually has sword fights? And how do I already know they don't use safety masks and rubber tips? They don't do anything half-assed. This would be real.

William pulls me to standing, his body warm and strong as he holds me. I'm shivering. Is this adrenaline? Am I in shock?

"You don't have to do this," I say between chattering teeth.

His brother hands him a sword, and he uses it to slice open the rope. I flinch, expecting that I would be cut by such a long, sharp blade, but my wrists are clean of blood. They're red and bruised, though.

William holds them in his larger hands, his jaw ticking. "He got to you."

I want to tell him that he got to me in time, that he managed to save me before I was raped...but I also know that the memory of Luca's weight, his attempt at a kiss, his hands opening my jeans will haunt me for a long time. Maybe forever.

The truth is I'm not sure I'll ever feel safe again.

William places a kiss on my forehead. It feels cleansing.

Then he pushes me gently back. Cormac takes a stance in front of me again. Asher stands in front of Matteo, as if keeping him from intervening to help his father—even though he looks as though all the fight has drained from him.

That leaves only William and Luca in the space, both armed.

They seem to hold the weapons with knowledge. Then again, what do I know about sword fighting? It happens in the very first scene of Romeo and Juliet, the drawing of swords. And look how that play ended. In tragedy.

"Please," I whisper to Cormac. "Make it stop."

He looks back at me, his eyes stormy. "This is his fight."

He's wrong, of course. It belongs to William. It also belongs to me.

They decide what happens because they're bigger and stronger. And older. They get to dictate to me, to protect me the way they choose. They get to strip me of choice in this moment. The knowledge rises like bile. There's nothing I can do to protect William from this.

The first clash of steel on steel echoes through the basement, a harsh, jarring sound that sets my teeth on edge. I feel like I can't watch, but I can't look away either. Two men circle each other, their movements fluid.

They both look skilled.

They both look deadly.

The fear in my gut turns to ice.

Luca lunges, his blade slicing through the air—and against William's arm. Blood wells up, staining the crisp white of his shirt. My heart stops, then starts again, pounding in my ears. I take a step forward, but Cormac holds me back.

"Trust him," he growls.

William doesn't even flinch. He just keeps fighting, his expression never changing. He's a machine, cold and calculating, his every move-ment precise. He forces Luca back, step by step, their blades clashing again and again.

The air fills with the harsh sound of their breathing, the ring of steel. Luca stumbles. William uses the moment to stab forward, slashing a precise line across his cheek, his right cheek, the same one where Luca hit me. He falls back, his sword clattering to the ground.

William stands over him, his blade at Luca's throat, chest heaving.

Luca looks up, his eyes wide with disbelief. He's not used to losing. As a narcissist, he probably assumed it couldn't happen. I didn't want this fight, but I can't help but be glad to see this evil man fall.

"Do it," he says, snarling.

Do what? He's already beaten?

The basement echoes with the harsh rasp of their breathing.

My blood runs cold. He wants William to kill

him.

He wants to make him a murderer.

Maybe he wants his head on fucking pike. Even his death has to be dramatic.

"No," I say, striding forward, putting a hand on William's chest. I'm close enough to the sword that it makes me feel sick, but I also can't let it happen this way. I don't care about what happens to Luca, but it will destroy something inside William to do this.

"He deserves it," Williams says.

"Don't you see? He wants this. Death by dramatic freaking duel. It would be the crowning achievement of the Shakespeare Society. Take it away from him. That's what he doesn't deserve."

William's sword presses against Luca's neck, the tip drawing a bead of blood.

Luca grits his teeth, his face a mask of defiance. "Finish it," he spits. "Are you going to let a little girl tell you what to do?"

William's lips curl into a sardonic smile. "Yes. I believe I am."

He lowers the sword, stepping back. His eyes meet mine, and the intensity in them sends a shiver down my spine. Relief floods through me like a tidal wave. He's bloodied, his shirt stained red, but he's alive.

Asher moves in to make sure that Luca doesn't get up.

"Anne." William's voice is a low rumble, a sound that makes my heart flutter.

"I was worried for you." The words escape my lips like a secret.

His hand cups my cheek, his thumb brushing away a tear I hadn't realized had fallen. His touch is electric, setting my skin on fire. "I wouldn't leave you."

You already did.

The words don't belong here, in this moment, even if they're true.

His lips claim mine in a kiss that's fierce and possessive. It's a brand, a promise. His tongue invades my mouth, tasting, exploring. I melt into him, my hands gripping his shirt, holding him close. The kiss deepens, becoming something wild and untamed. I can feel his heart pounding against my chest, echoing my own.

He pulls back, his breath ragged.

Luca stirs, his body trembling as he pushes himself up from the ground. My heart stops. His face drips blood, making him a gory mess, defiance in his eyes. Cormac steps forward. "Thank God. Even I couldn't kick a man when he's down. So I'm glad you got up."

Before Luca can fully stand, Cormac's fist connects with his jaw. The sound is sickening, a brutal crack that makes me wince.

"That's for leaving college students in fucking fountains," he says over the prone body.

Luca doesn't stir.

There's only one student that's happened to recently, and that's Daisy. The memory of her, soaked and shivering, flashes through my mind, making me shiver.

William's eyes search mine. "He touched you."

I nod, unable to find the words. He did more than touch my body. He dirtied my soul.

His thumb brushes my lower lip, a soft, tender touch that sends a shiver down my spine. "You're going to heal. That's a goddamn promise."

Heal. I don't know what that would look like, especially since my wounds go so much deeper than tonight. He takes my hand, his fingers intertwining with mine. His grip is firm, steady. He leads me away from the chaos, away from the violence. Away from Luca and Matteo, who are now nothing more than shadows in the night.

We step out into the cool night air, the stars shining brightly above us. The night is quiet, peaceful. It's as if the world has been holding its breath, waiting for us. It looks almost pretty, as if this is a romantic date instead of a bizarre rescue. How perverse. And how appropriate to everything that our relationship has been.

He turns to me, his eyes black in the moonlight. "You're safe now."

"I've never been safe. I doubt it's going to start now."

He leans in, his forehead resting on mine.

The sound of sirens cuts through the tension, growing louder as they approach. William's hold on me tightens, his voice a low rumble in my ear. "Hold on, brave heart."

The ambulance pulls up outside, its lights casting a red and blue glow through the open basement door. Paramedics rush in, their faces set in professional concern. They ask if there are injuries inside. Injuries like a man cut with a sword and then knocked out cold.

"There's a man inside who needs medical attention, but she needs to be looked at first." He uses his professor voice, which means they listen.

"I'm not that hurt."

"No arguments. I'm about two seconds away from locking you away where no one can find you, kidnap you, drag you into cold fucking cellars."

I open my mouth to protest, but the look in his eyes stops me. He's not just concerned; he's scared. Scared for me. The realization sends a warm rush through me, and I find myself nodding, acquiescing, allowing medics to press ice against my cheek.

CHAPTER TWENTY-FOUR

Dropped Out

I FULLY EXPECTED to be taken back to campus.

My dorm room, most likely.

Or the provost's house, although William hasn't lived there for many months. I would even accept the bell tower, except that Mary is using it now.

Perhaps that's why we end up at a gorgeous modern home that's apparently owned by Cormac. It's all angles and glass, its sleekness a contrast to the craggy shore behind it.

I'm a person who will prefer old things to the new, who wants dusty paper instead of shiny screens, but I can't deny the luxury of this uber-modern palace. The bedroom I'm in has a balcony. It overlooks a place where rock juts into sky, along with the riotous symphony of crashing waves.

Physically, I feel better after some pain meds

and a hot shower. My body throbs gently, a reminder of the ordeal I've been through, but it's manageable.

Emotionally, though, I'm a mess.

I swing my legs out of bed, the cool wooden floor sending a jolt through my system. I'm wearing an oversized T-shirt, one that says *Tanglewood University*. It's comforting, a touchstone to something I know in a foreign land.

This place is a world away from the cramped dorm rooms.

The low rumble of masculine voices drifts upstairs as William handles the mundane details of violence and retribution. I turn away from the window, my heart pounding in my chest. I'm safe, I know that, but the fear, the uncertainty, it's still there. It's still real. And it's not going away anytime soon.

The door to the bedroom creaks open.

Daisy steps into the room, her blue eyes filled with concern. She doesn't say a word, just crosses the room and pulls me into a tight hug. I stiffen at first, still raw from everything that's happened, but her warmth seeps into me, and I relax, melting into her embrace.

She pulls back, her hands on my shoulders, and looks me over. "You're okay," she says, more a statement than a question.

I nod, not trusting my voice.

She wraps a blanket around my shoulders and tucks it in around me, her movements brisk and efficient. I want to tell her not to worry over me, not to fuss, but the truth is that I'm grateful to be the recipient of her care.

"Drink this," she says, pressing a hot cup of tea into my hands. I take a sip, the heat and sweetness of chamomile tea with honey warming me from the inside out.

She sits down on the bed next to me, her leg pressed against mine. She takes my free hand in hers, her thumb tracing circles on the back of my hand. It's a small gesture, but it anchors me, keeps me present in the moment.

"You don't have to talk about it," she says. "But I'm here if you want to."

I shake my head, unable to speak.

She seems to understand, chatting about inconsequential things, filling the silence with her warm voice. She talks about her latest engineering project, about the new café that's opened up near campus, about how Mary is learning everything about the "outside world" through TikTok. I can't imagine that being my first introduction to regular people.

I let her words wash over me. It's comforting, this semblance of normalcy. It reminds me that there's a world outside of the chaos I've been living in, a world where people go to cafés and work on engineering projects and learn about social media.

As she talks, she starts to brush my hair, her fingers gentle as they work out the tangles. It's a soothing rhythm, and I feel my eyes start to drift closed. I'm safe here, with her. I can let go, just for a moment.

Even as I relax, a tension remains in me, a coiled spring.

I have a place to sleep tonight, but what about tomorrow? What about when I have to face the world again, when I have to face the cold reality of my situation?

She seems to sense my tension, her hand stilling in my hair. "It's okay," she says, her voice barely above a whisper. "You're okay. Don't think about it."

I take a deep breath, trying to obey her.

Trying to believe that everything will be okay.

There's a knock at the door, a sharp sound that cuts through the warmth.

Daisy and I exchange a glance, her blue eyes reflecting the same uncertainty I feel. She moves to the door, her steps hesitant. I clutch the blanket tighter around my shoulders, my heart pounding in my chest.

Daisy cracks open the door. She stiffens. "Absolutely not."

Then I hear a familiar voice, urgent and pleading. "I need to know she's okay."

Carlisle.

My breath hitches, a mix of emotions surging through me. Relief, anger, confusion. I hadn't realized how much I missed my friend.

Daisy looks back at me, a question in her eyes.

I nod, a small, jerky movement.

With clear reluctance, she steps back to let her in.

Carlisle stands in the doorway, her usually bright and gorgeous appearance replaced with a look of desolation. Her eyes are red-rimmed, her cheeks streaked with tears. She's wearing a hoodie and jeans, her hair pulled back into a messy ponytail.

She looks like she's been through hell and back.

I'm sure I look worse.

Since Daisy looks ready to rip into her, I head onto the balcony, where there are two chairs that look modern but are surprisingly comfortable. I sink into one of them with a sigh.

Carlisle sits in the other one, leaned forward, hands pressed together as if in prayer.

Praying to the tumultuous ocean, perhaps.

We sit in a long silence that's surprisingly companionable.

After what happened I would have expected there to be more awkwardness. Instead I might even feel *more* at ease with her than before. She's more human to me now. More real. I suppose knowing secrets has a way of creating intimacy.

It makes me wonder if that's what really started the Shakespeare Society, the human need for intimacy. College is not a place that has a lot of that. Oh, there are lots of people. Too many people, really. People come here from all over the city, all over the state. They even come here from all over the world.

They leave their families, their friends behind in pursuit of…what?

Higher learning, perhaps.

Powerful career prospects. Maybe.

But on some level, we came here, all of us, seeking a new family, one who made more sense than the one we were born to. And the secret society, while toxic, while dangerous, while absolutely terrible, did provide that for some people.

What is the alternative?

I don't know the answer to that, but I do know that humans weren't made to be alone. I know that now, now that I've fallen in love, regardless of whether that love is doomed.

"So," Carlisle says, her tone droll, "anything interesting happen to you lately? Like, did you try out a new mascara? Or did they serve something besides meatloaf at the Hathaway cafeteria on a Wednesday?"

Despite everything, a smile touches my lips. "Oh, you know. Same old, same old."

She snickers. Then sighs. "Is there someone I can kill for you? Because I feel like that might make you feel better. And it would definitely make me feel better."

"No murders," I tell her.

"You're too nice. I've always thought that about you."

I shake my head with a small grin. "I've learned how to be bloodthirsty, actually, but I already have a knight who slayed the dragon."

She sobers. "You think you know why I wanted to be friends with you."

"It's because I was the only person here who wasn't worshipping at your feet, who was ignorant enough not to know who you were. And everyone likes a little variety in their life."

"The reason why I wanted to be friends with you is because you're an interesting person, a nice person, a *good* person."

I shake my head. It's not that I think I'm evil. I've looked into the face of that recently enough that I can't make that mistake. But being insulted and knocked around by your parents your whole life will do a number on the brain. It will make you believe that you don't deserve anything—not true friends, not good grades. Not even a scholarship.

"I knew you wouldn't believe me, but it's true. Though I did have an ulterior motive."

"Ha," I say.

"It's not that you didn't care about me. It's that you *did* care about me. As a human. All those people, the ones who follow me around campus, who ask for autographs, who post my pictures online, they don't care about me. They don't even know me."

Shit. "I'm sorry."

"Don't apologize, but most of them don't like me. They actually hate me."

My heart clenches. Everyone loves Carlisle Storm. That's why they're so obsessed with her, right? Then again, it's possible to be obsessed with someone you hate. The certainty in her voice gives me chills. "There are going to be assholes," I try.

She shakes her head. "I'm not even talking about the trolls or the religious fanatics who tell me I'm going to hell. I mean *all* of them. The ones who want to be my friend, especially. They hate me because I shouldn't have this fame, and they know it. The fact that my voice sounds a certain way, the fact that I look a certain way, the music they play on the radio, it was all given to me. I didn't earn it."

My brows draw together. What she's saying feels important. It feels vital, but I also don't understand it. "I've never seen you on tour, or in the recording studio, or rehearsing, or writing songs, but I don't imagine that it's easy."

She shrugs. "There are a hundred more talented people in the music department, people with more range, with stronger voices, with more creativity."

"Bullshit."

"You're right, though. It's not easy. Sometimes I just want to give it all up. But then my mom calls me and reminds me that it's not actually an option."

My heart clenches. "I'm sorry."

"No, I don't want your sympathy. I don't deserve it. That's my point." She tugs on one of her long black curls, a nervous habit. "I'm only bringing it up to show you that I value our friendship. And if I've lost it over this, then that's nothing less than I deserve. But you were never just someone who I knew, who I liked because you didn't read the gossip or listen to pop music. You aren't a friend of convenience. You're someone I care about greatly, someone I—" Her voice cracks. "Someone who I'll miss for a long time, if this is the last time we see each other."

Tears prick my eyes. Am I supposed to stay mad at her? I can't seem to find any anger inside me, not when what she's saying feels like the truth, not when I've seen the alternative. Making mistakes happens to anyone, but most people double down. There are people who live their entire life with lies, even as they smile to your face. Even as they stab a gilt dagger in your back. And I know what kind of person I prefer.

I want friends who make mistakes.

Who apologize.

I don't want people who are secretly plotting to kill you.

"Don't talk like that," I tell her, my voice husky. "This isn't the last time we're going to see each other. Of course not. Just because we're going through a rough patch doesn't mean we're not still friends."

"Damn it," she says, wiping her eyes. "You're being too nice again."

"I just…wish I could understand you better. I know what the gossip accounts have cost you, how painful they've been. How could you become one of them? I understand the way it started, but why keep it going?"

She looks out at the ocean, which roars in windy abandon. It's gorgeous to look at. Terrifying to consider being asea. That's what the world of fame looks like to me. "God," she says. "Do professors make more than I thought? This is an incredible view."

"He might do work on the side. I mean, the literature professors do that, too, but it usually doesn't pay as well. Maybe engineering pays better."

"Like I said, it started as a joke. I would post and then forget about it. But then they'd come after me again, and I don't know, it just felt like if I posted, half as a parody, half as self-flagellation… It felt like I was controlling the narrative somehow."

"Oh, Carlisle."

"I think I was trying to understand my enemies. I was becoming them, just so I could learn not to hate them. I didn't want that feeling to eat me up inside."

I think back to Thorne's terrible ambition, the way she was so desperate to succeed that she would hurt anyone to get ahead. She used men, she hurt women, even as she understood that she perpetuated the cycle of privilege. Where did that drive come from? Hatred? Was she so bitter about the fact that women get fewer opportunities in this field—and in most fields, if we're honest—that she felt justified doing anything to succeed? Even illegal, dangerous, harmful things? Even murder?

No. That's giving her too much credit.

It's like Ms. O'Connor said. *You can't always argue for the best possible interpretation. Sometimes people are just wrong. Sometimes they're just cruel. That's the part of Shakespeare you never wanted to face.*

It would be easy for me to hate Thorne, but Carlisle is right. It would eat me up inside. It would turn me into some other version of Thorne, one who's bitter.

I can't let that happen.

I've worked too hard to escape the Society.

I can't become what they are, what they were.

"Did it help you understand them," I ask, "in the end?"

She nods, looking thoughtful. "Weirdly enough, yes. What happens when you start posting and people are following you is that people start talking back to you. Comments and DMs. They started sending me information. Gossip about me, that I knew was a lie, but how would other accounts know that?"

"They should verify their sources."

"And then there was the gossip about other people. Gossip is just a term for news, when you think about it. I got this tip about how a guy on the football team had roofied this girl who was still in high school. The coach was trying to cover it up. Sports is big money for the university, so they were hoping it went away."

"Oh God."

"I asked around. Used my position as Carlisle Storm to get information that I might not have had otherwise. And then I posted it. Everything blew up from there. Things started happening. The player got suspended. The coach got fired. The school made a stern statement."

"That's incredible."

"It didn't permanently fix anything, of course.

There are more players to do horrible things and more coaches to cover them up. But it was…something. Something that mattered. Something in the right direction. It was more than I could do without the account."

I can understand the allure too well.

"I kept posting. Some of it I would find myself, but most of it came through other people. And this part was a surprise—the number of people who want me to post about them. They'll share their own gossip as part of a popularity game."

"Wow."

"Some people offered to pay me to post stories. Or to sponsor ads. I didn't take it, of course, but it took on a life of its own. And that was important, too. It was an identity. A secret one, something that belonged to me and me alone, something that could not be judged, objectified, or monetized by my mother. No one could complain that Tanglewood Tea looks like it gained five pounds. They didn't speculate if I was sleeping with someone as a PR stunt. The secret made it feel safe."

"I understand."

She looks unconvinced. "Do you?"

"I understand wanting to be safe."

"I couldn't actually be in that many places, at parties and things like that, and be inconspicuous, so most of what I posted came through other sources. I did work to verify them, but even so, it wasn't a guarantee that everything I said was one hundred percent true."

"It was true in my case," I say softly.

She flinches. "Yes."

"I looked up the post again. I saw the way you worded it, the way you tried to protect my name, keep me out of it. I know that you were thinking about what was best for me. And that, in your own way, with your own power, you were trying to keep me safe, too."

"I failed."

"You can't save the world, Carlisle. What happened to me is the result of evil people. What you did could protect other students, ones who don't have the power to say no. I don't want you to stop posting because of what happened."

"It doesn't matter. It's over."

"No, you're doing real good in the school. This is important."

"I'm done at Tanglewood University. So I can't exactly post the gossip."

"What do you mean?"

"I dropped out."

"What?"

"I'm going on tour."

I blink. "But you said you hate touring."

"It's what my mom wants, what she always wants."

She's younger than me, having been home-schooled so that she could perform as a child. That's how she got into college two years ago. "Aren't you eighteen now?"

"I don't have the heart to keep telling her no."

Damn. I wish I didn't understand that. It doesn't actually matter, when you're a child, how unreasonable your parents are. You just want them to love you. Even if that means working in a diner and giving them all your money for a cancer that was never real.

And, apparently, even if that means going on a worldwide tour you hate.

"Maybe you can come and finish your classes after."

"There's really nothing here for me. You'll have graduated by then."

"You wanted your degree."

"I wanted the dream, the college experience, like Glee mixed with The Queen's Gambit, but it was never that. It wasn't even just the students who hated me. It was the professors, too. They're musicians, too, of course. They resented that I had the fame, even though they're the ones teaching me. I need to stop putting myself through that."

"I know you're not ready to hear this right now, but I'm telling you, education is a right. You deserve one. You deserve to be here as much as anyone."

She shakes her head, her lower lip trembling.

"Maybe later," I whisper.

I meant what I said. We all deserve this. Scholarship or not. Pop star or not. Those who want to learn should always have a place at Tanglewood University. That's what the people who started secret societies don't understand. We already belong.

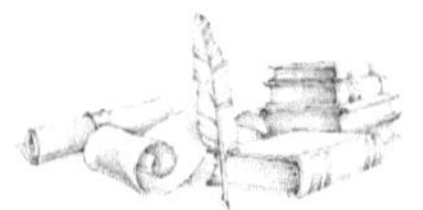

CHAPTER TWENTY-FIVE

Insatiable Curiosity

Daisy

I TIPTOE DOWN the grand staircase, my heart pounding in my chest. The modern chandelier overhead casts a soft glow, guiding my way. I'm almost at the front door when a deep voice cuts through the silence.

"Going somewhere?"

I freeze, my hand hovering over the doorknob. Cormac stands in the shadows, his tall, muscular frame leaning against the wall. His eyes, dark and intense, meet mine.

"I, uh, was just going to catch the bus," I stammer, my cheeks flushing. I'm not usually one to be at a loss for words, but something about Cormac leaves me flustered.

He pushes off the wall and steps into the light. His rugged features, usually set in a stern expression, soften slightly as he looks at me. "It's late," he says, his voice a low rumble. "And it's not safe."

I lift my chin. "I can take care of myself."

A small smirk tugs at the corner of his mouth. "I don't doubt that." He takes a step closer, his gaze never leaving mine. "But you don't have to. Not while you're here."

I swallow hard, my heart fluttering in my chest. This is dangerous territory. Cormac is Anne's professor's brother, and I'm…well, I'm just Daisy. The engineering student with dark secrets and insatiable curiosity. That's what drives me to learn about electrical currents and gears. It's also what makes me fascinated with this man.

"Look, I appreciate your concern," I say, trying to keep my voice steady. "But I really need to go."

He takes another step closer, his proximity sending a shiver down my spine. "Why are you running?"

I open my mouth to respond, but no words come out. The truth is, I don't know why I'm running. Or maybe I do, and I just don't want to admit it.

Cormac reaches out, his hand gently cupping my cheek. His touch is warm, his thumb brushing softly against my skin. "You don't have to run.

Not from me."

My breath hitches, my heart pounding wildly. This is wrong, isn't it? He's forbidden, off-limits. But then why does it feel so right?

I lean into his touch, my eyes fluttering closed. When I open them again, Cormac is even closer, his breath mingling with mine.

"Daisy," he whispers, his voice husky.

My heart skips a beat, my body yearning for his touch. But before I can respond, a noise from upstairs startles us both. We jump apart, our moment shattered.

Cormac clears his throat, his expression once again stern. "You should stay here tonight," he says, his voice gruff. "We can talk more in the morning."

"You don't get to tell me what to do."

"Don't I?" His eyes glint dangerously in the dim light of the foyer. His voice is a low growl, a warning that sends a shiver down my spine. "I told you what happens to lost little lambs who don't stay with the flock."

I should be afraid, and I am, but there's something else coursing through my veins. Excitement. A thrill that I can't quite explain. Maybe it's the remnants of my upbringing, the echoes of domination and submission that were drilled into me from a young age. Or maybe it's just the raw, primal power that Cormac exudes.

"Well, you certainly took your sweet time rounding up this little lamb," I retort, my voice steady despite the pounding in my chest. "Anne was in trouble, and you were nowhere to be found."

Cormac's jaw tightens, a muscle twitching in his cheek. "I had things to take care of," he says, his voice a low rumble. "And I'm not the one who let her wander off in the first place."

I bristle at the accusation, but I can't deny the truth in his words. I should have been more careful, should have kept a closer eye on Anne. But I won't let him see me flinch. "Well, you're certainly making up for lost time now, aren't you?" I snap back. "Playing the big, bad wolf."

A smirk tugs at the corner of his mouth, and he takes a step closer. I can feel the heat radiating off his body, can see the stubble that lines his jaw. "You have no idea, little lamb," he murmurs, his voice a low growl that sends a shiver down my spine.

Defiance sparks. I should be intimidated, should be cowering in the face of his power. Fuck that. "And you have no idea what I'm capable of."

Cormac's eyes flash, and for a moment, I

think he's going to pounce. "Pray that I never find out." A veil drops over his dark eyes. "You've been a good friend to Anne."

The sudden shift in his demeanor catches me off guard. I blink, taken aback by the unexpected kindness in his voice. "She's been a good friend to me," I say, my voice soft. "Thank you for helping her. For helping both of us."

"For helping," he repeats, his voice flat.

"You know, for letting her stay here to recuperate. And for rescuing her."

Cormac's voice is a low rumble, a warning that sends a shiver down my spine. "It wasn't a rescue, little lamb. We were capturing her for William. He should know better than to touch a student. He might not want to let her go."

I glance up at him, my heart pounding in my chest. There's a darkness in his eyes, a hunger that sends a thrill coursing through my veins. As if he's thinking about touching a student. Not just any student. Me.

I take a step closer, my breath hitching as his scent fills my nostrils. He smells like pine and earth, a wild, untamed scent that makes my heart race. Cormac growls, a sound that vibrates through me, and suddenly, I'm pressed against the wall, his body caging mine.

I look up at him, my eyes wide, my lips parted. I hope he'll kiss me. I want him to kiss me. But when he leans down, his lips press against my forehead, a chaste kiss that leaves me aching for more.

He sets me gently, but firmly, away from him. "Run home, little lamb. You won't like what will happen if I catch you."

I swallow hard, my body trembling with a mix of fear and desire. I know I should run, should flee from this dangerous man and the wild, untamed feelings he stirs within me. But my feet remain rooted to the ground, my eyes locked on his.

Cormac's gaze sweeps over me, his expression darkening. "I said run," he growls, his voice a low rumble that sends a shiver down my spine. "Now."

I take a deep breath, my heart pounding in my chest. And then, with a burst of speed, I dart past him, my feet flying over the ground as I race toward the safety of the bus route, of campus, of the empty dorm room.

What would have happened if I stayed?

I glance back over my shoulder, my heart racing. But Cormac is nowhere to be seen. I take a deep breath, trying to calm my racing heart, and step inside, the door closing behind me with a soft click.

I lean back against the door, my body trembling with a mix of fear and desire. And as I close my eyes, all I can see is Cormac's face, his dark eyes burning into mine. All I can feel is the press of his lips against my forehead, the rumble of his growl vibrating through me.

And I know, without a doubt, that I'm in deep, deep trouble.

CHAPTER TWENTY-SIX

Silent Poetry

D AISY HEADS BACK to campus. She has an advanced calculus exam. Even the idea of which makes me shudder. As well as Mary to look after. It worries me, how overloaded she is, mother henning her sister as well as me.

We both carefully avoided the idea of *after*.

After this semester, when the scholarship has run out.

The bed in here feels like a dream. I've always heard money can't buy happiness, but if it can buy mattresses that feel like clouds, that's pretty close to the same thing. After three and a half years on a lumpy dorm mattress, my body sinks into a long sleep.

When I wake, a thick fog washes out the landscape, making it more forbidding.

I head downstairs, where Cormac stands at a counter, drinking coffee.

His eyebrows push together when he sees me. "You shouldn't be out of bed."

The Stratford brothers are entirely too comfortable telling me what to do. Or what *not* to do. Does that come naturally to them as professors? Or as men? Either way, I'm no longer inclined to listen. "I'm going for a walk."

His eyes flick down to my feet, where I already have my sneakers on. And then back up again. I can see him considering bodily blocking me from leaving.

"I'm *going* for a walk," I tell him. "I need some air."

"William will be here soon."

I want to ask him where he's been, but I manage to stop myself. Actually, I expected William to join me in that cloud of a bed. It couldn't feel cold, not with the blankets that cocooned me. It did feel lonely, though.

That's probably the part that money can't buy.

Love.

Outside, wind whips around me. Icy tendrils tugging at my clothes and hair.

It's a relief to know that William will be here soon.

And embarrassing to care.

It feels humiliating to wonder where William has been, especially after spending so long looking for a grave that didn't exist. It represented the way I wasn't important enough to grieve him. Or as I know now, that I wasn't important enough to entrust with his secret.

I'm standing on the edge of a cliff.

A literal one. A metaphorical one, too.

The landscape sprawls out before me, a wild and untamed vista that steals my breath away. Craggy rocks jut out from the heath, their dark silhouettes stark against the muted greens and browns of the moors.

The waterfront is a churning mass of white-caps and foam, the sea battling against the land in an eternal struggle. It's a scene straight out of *Macbeth*, a place where witchcraft and treachery seem not only possible but inevitable.

Or maybe that's just my overwrought imagination working.

Where will I go next semester?

Maybe I can be a roadie on Carlisle's new tour.

No, I would be a terrible roadie. I get carsick.

Maybe I can run away with Mary. We can both go undercover with new names, as if we're witnesses in a protection program. Except that I am tired of hiding.

There's home, of course.

The place that never felt like home.

I can become a librarian. I would have to clean up bodily fluids from strangers and mother random children who are ignored by the system, but at least I would get to cover the books with protective plastic coating.

I don't want to go back home.

My heart pounds in my chest, my emotions a storm that rivals the one raging around me. I came here to think, to clear my head, to try to make sense of the chaos that my life has become. But standing here, on the precipice, all I feel is a deep, aching sense of uncertainty.

I love him.

It's not a welcome truth, but it's true just the same.

I love William Stratford—his strength, his passion, his presence. I love the way he makes me feel alive, the way he challenges me, the way he touches me. The thought of leaving him, of leaving Tanglewood, feels like a physical pain.

But I can't rely on him.

Not for money, not for security, not for any-thing.

I've seen the dark path that leads down, seen

it in the hollowed-out eyes of my mother, in the clenched fists of my father. I've seen what happens when you depend on someone else for your happiness, your safety, your life.

I can't live that way.

The wind howls, a mournful sound that echoes the turmoil within me. I wrap my arms around myself, a futile attempt to ward off the cold, to hold myself together. But it's no use. I'm coming apart at the seams, my heart and mind pulling me in opposite directions, threatening to tear me in two.

I think about the university, about the hallowed halls and the whispered secrets, about the dreams and the promises that brought me here. About the Society, about the darkness that lurks beneath the surface, about the power and the corruption that have taken root like a cancer.

And I think about him. About William.

About the way he looks at me, the way he touches me, the way he makes me feel. About the love that burns between us, a flame that threatens to consume us both. About the secrets he keeps, the darkness that clings to him like a shadow. There's a power around him, a control he exerts over me—and that's the true danger that lurks beneath his smooth, seductive surface, how badly

I want to submit to that power.

I want to let him take care of me.

And then what would I be?

No more independent than Daisy or Mary or any of the women who live in the cult.

The wind screams around me, a wild and primal sound that calls to something deep within me. I close my eyes, letting the noise, the chaos, the uncertainty wash over me. For a brief blink of time, I become part of the cliff, the sea, the wild and untamed landscape.

A voice breaks through the wind. "Anne."

It brings me back to this moment. He brings me back to myself.

What a heartbreaking thing to realize.

I turn, my heart pounding in my chest, my breath held in my throat. And I face the voice, the darkness, the danger, the threat.

Professor Stratford stands before me, a towering figure against the wild backdrop of the moors. His dark hair is disheveled, tossed by the wind, and his eyes burn with an intensity that makes my breath catch. He's dressed in all black, the stark color accentuating the muscled lines of his body. His shoulders are broad, his chest powerful, tapering down to a lean waist. He looks every inch the brooding hero, a man carved from the very storm that rages around us.

He strides toward me, his steps sure and deliberate, eating up the distance between us. His jaw is set, his expression determined. There's a sense of barely leashed power about him, a raw, primal energy that sends a shiver down my spine.

I wrap my arms around myself, a futile attempt to ward off the cold, to protect myself from the intensity of his gaze.

He stops in front of me, close enough that I can feel the heat radiating off his body. His eyes search mine. "What are you doing out here?"

"Thinking."

"Have you come to any conclusions?"

That I need you too much. Enough that I have to let you go for my own good.

His eyebrows come together, reminding me of his brother. Which probably means he's about to tell me something I can't do. "You can't leave."

"I needed air."

"I mean you can't leave Tanglewood."

Oh. That. "We can talk about it later."

He reaches out, his hand cupping my cheek. His touch is gentle, a stark contrast to the storm that rages around us, to the fire that burns in his eyes. "You're right," he says, his thumb brushing against my skin. "You were right when you said I didn't trust you."

Surprise makes my heart skip a beat. "I didn't think you'd ever admit that."

"I didn't want to," he admits. "But it's true. If I had trusted you more, I would have told you. I would have let you risk yourself the same way I risked myself. Because God knows my greatest fear happened anyway. You were at the hands of a madman for fucking hours. I let that happen to you, so I can't act like what I did was protection. All it did was take your choice away. I'm sorry."

I didn't think he'd apologize, either. Our power dynamic had been one-sided. Carlisle was right. And like William, I didn't want to admit that. Not that he forced me to have sex, the way she worried. But we also weren't a regular dating couple. The age difference, the fact that he was my professor. And how badly, how deeply I longed to be taken care of. While at the same time knowing I couldn't really accept it.

"I'm sorry, too," I say, my voice hoarse.

"Don't."

"It's okay," I tell him, wanting it to be true.

"Don't you fucking dare. I will apologize every day for the rest of my life, if I have to, but don't you dare talk about us as if we're over."

My throat feels tight. "I don't know what else

we can do. I'm leaving Tanglewood. For a semester, at least. And for the summer. I'm not sure how long it will take to get fixed. Or how long it will take for me to save up the money on my own."

His hand slides to the back of my neck, his fingers tangling in my hair. He leans in, his forehead resting against mine. "You can rely on me."

I shake my head, a small, desperate movement. "You don't understand."

His grip tightens, his fingers pressing into my skin. His eyes burn into mine, their dark depths swirling with determination. "I understand that you're scared," he says, his voice a low growl. "I understand that you're hurt, but I also understand this."

He leans in, his lips brushing against mine. The touch is soft, gentle, a whisper of a kiss. But it sends a jolt of electricity coursing through my body, a spark that ignites a fire deep within me.

"I understand that you're mine. And I'm not letting you go. Not now. Not ever."

I gasp, my heart pounding in my chest. His words, his touch, his presence—it's all too much. It's overwhelming, consuming, a storm that threatens to sweep me away. But even as I struggle to resist, even as I fight against the pull that he exerts, I know that I'm lost.

The wind whips around us, but I barely feel the cold. Not with William's body so close to mine, his hand still tangled in my hair, his forehead pressed against mine. His eyes burn into me, their dark depths swirling with an intensity that steals my breath.

"You're mine," he says again, his voice a low growl that sends a shiver down my spine. "Do you think it only goes one way? I'm yours. Completely. Irrevocably."

I shake my head, a small, desperate movement. "I can't rely on you. I can't depend on you. I won't be like her. I won't be like my mother. You don't know what it was like."

His grip tightens, his fingers pressing into my skin. His eyes never leave mine, their dark depths swirling with determination and desperation. "I can guess from the way you've had to make your own way in the world from such a young age. I can guess from the way it's a surprise to you whenever anyone helps you in even the smallest way."

I try to pull away, but his hold is firm, unyielding. "Then you'll know why this can't work. You have more money, more power, more *everything.* It would always be uneven."

He flinches, his eyes closing briefly. When they open again, they're filled with pain, with regret. "Do you think that means anything to me?"

I shake my head, tears stinging my eyes. "It means something to *me*."

His lips crash into mine, silencing my words, stealing my breath. The kiss is fierce, desperate, a wild and primal claim that sends a jolt of electricity coursing through my body. His arms wrap around me, pulling me tight against him, his body a solid, unyielding wall of muscle and heat.

He breaks the kiss, his breath ragged, his eyes wild. "You can trust me. I'll be your rock, your shelter, your sanctuary. I'll be whatever you need, whatever you want. Stay. That's all I need from you, because if you leave, I'm truly dead."

I shake my head, tears spilling down my cheeks. "I can't stay here. I can't—"

His hands cup my face, his thumbs brushing away my tears. His eyes burn into mine, their dark depths swirling with desperation and despair. "Then we'll go. We'll leave Tanglewood, leave the university, leave all this behind. I'll leave behind the fucking money. I'll leave behind my name. We'll start fresh, somewhere new, somewhere you can feel safe."

I stare at him, my heart pounding in my chest. It would be too much to ever ask of him, but even the idea… "You would do that? You would leave all this behind? For me?"

He nods, his jaw set, his expression determined. "I would do anything for you. Anything. I love you. I love you more than anything, more than anyone. I love you more than my life, more than my breath, more than my own fucking soul."

I gasp, his words sending a shock wave through my body, through my heart, through my very being. "William—"

His hands tighten on my face, his eyes burning into mine. "I love you more than Shakespeare."

A shaky laugh escapes me. "Don't."

"I didn't devote my life to the study because of goddamn iambic pentameter. It was only ever to describe what I felt inside, what I dreamed about, the love I felt for you before we even met."

A broken sound escapes me.

I stare at him, my heart pounding, my breath caught in my throat. His words, his touch, his presence—it's all too much. It's overwhelming, consuming, a storm that threatens to sweep me away. But even as I struggle to resist, I know that

I'm lost.

His dark eyes burn with promise. "I found you in the Pinnacle, where you were a goddamn dream. A forbidden one. Too young. Too risky. And then you walked into my classroom, and I knew that you would be worth the risk. Worth everything. Would I be willing to give it up? In a heartbeat."

"You don't have to leave," I say, my voice wavering.

"Anne—"

"You can stay…with me. Stand with me. Fight with me. Love with me."

He closes his eyes, his breath ragged, his body tense. When he opens them again, they're filled with a fierce determination, a fire that burns hot and bright, a reflection of the love that blazes between us. "Yes," he says, his voice a low growl, a vow that sends a shiver down my spine. "God, yes."

"Because I love you, too."

I lean into him, surrendering to his touch, to his kiss, to his keeping. There's a language between our bodies.

Words are powerful, but they can't touch this.

We write silent poetry with every heartbeat.

Maybe that's why I read Shakespeare, too.

Maybe he was the dream I had from those early days in the library, having my bruises tended by Ms. O'Connor. And Shakespeare? He was the rope we used to find each other, hand over hand, through the storms of our lives, each of us pulling closer, until we finally met.

CHAPTER TWENTY-SEVEN

Thine Own Hand

Anne

I WALK INTO the classroom, the familiar hum of fluorescent lights buzzing overhead. The room looks so ordinary, so untouched by the chaos that has swept through Tanglewood. Rows of desks stretch out before me, their faux wood surfaces worn smooth by years of use. It's almost as if nothing has changed, as if the world hasn't been turned upside down and shaken like a snow globe.

The chalkboard at the front has Professor Oglevy's familiar scrawl: *Final Exam.*

Dean Morris convinced her to come back. Rumor has it that she was having a torrid love affair with a scholar younger than her. It began when she was guest lecturing in Italy. Now her skin is definitely tan and glowing, though her frizzy hair is a comforting halo around her face.

My heart thumps steadily in my chest, a familiar rhythm of pre-exam jitters. It's a strange comfort, this feeling. It's normal, unlike the surreal events of the past weeks. I've faced actual death, yet here I am, nervous about a final exam.

It's absurd, really, but it's a testament to the human spirit, I suppose. We find normalcy where we can, even in the midst of madness.

I choose one of the many desks that have the chairs attached. Too small. A little rusted. Uncomfortable as hell but I'll miss them.

At least, I'll miss them if I pass the final exam.

I pull out my pencils, their sharpened tips promising control. I set them down carefully, lining them up next to the shrink-wrapped "blue book" that will hold my words, my thoughts, my ticket to graduation.

All around me, my classmates are doing the same.

Tension vibrates in the air, a mix of anxiety and anticipation. We all have one last hurdle before we can call ourselves graduates. I glance over at Tyler, who's sitting a few rows away. He catches my eye and smiles, and I manage a small one back.

I scan the room one last time, my gaze snagging on the empty seat near the back. Matteo's seat. A pang of something—not quite regret, not quite relief—echoes through me. He's gone, dropped out, or so the rumors say. Maybe he's with his father, living it up overseas, far away from Tanglewood and the mess they both created.

Good riddance, I think, but the sentiment feels hollow.

Professor Oglevy pulls out a stack of papers from her worn leather satchel, the final exam that will decide our fates. She sets them down on her desk, her eyes scanning the room.

"Good morning, class," she says. "Today is the day you've all been waiting for. The final exam." She pauses, her gaze sweeping over us once more. "It's been a tumultuous semester, or so I've heard. I'm gone only a few semesters and everything falls apart."

She looks around, her gaze landing on me.

"Did Shakespeare write Macbeth? What a question for a final exam. As if his authorship could ever be in question. Though I suppose we can't be too shocked, now that we know the truth about Isolde."

She isn't even referring to the Shakespeare Society. Or the scholarship fund. Instead, she's referring to a paper that was published by a major academic paper…only to be retracted a week later. She managed to convince a researcher working in

England to claim he found the extant manuscript, since they would require a source.

It was huge news in the Shakespearean world when it hit.

And then someone found the reference I'd hidden to Lanternleaf Legends.

A modern easter egg that definitively proved it to be false.

The supposed source immediately recanted.

Isolde Thorne's name became a source of rage and then mockery.

And of course, she now knows I'm the one who wrought her downfall.

That feels good in a karmic sort of way, but it doesn't actually solve my problem.

Professor Oglevy sighs. "And yet, it was also the final exam question given to you at the beginning of the year, the one you have worked on. So is it unfair to change it now? I decided that it's kinder to allow you to complete your work as you prepared for it. Your argument, whether for or against authorship, as a certain, now disgraced professor told you, will be assigned randomly."

She hands out single sheets of paper, one per desk.

Argue against Shakespeare's Authorship of Macbeth, mine says.

My stomach drops. It's the question I dreaded.

The one I was sure Professor Thorne would have given me, *not* randomly.

Now she's gone in disgrace…but it's still mine to answer.

At least, as Professor Oglevy said, I did prepare for it.

"You have two hours to complete your essay," she says, her voice echoing in the large classroom. "Make it compelling, make it insightful. Make me believe your words."

I flip the exam notebook open.

Blank pages stare back at me.

Deep breath.

Then I begin writing. Words flow from my mind to my hand, a dance of letters forming sentences, paragraphs, ideas.

I lose myself in the words, in the world of *Macbeth*.

The clock ticks away the minutes, but I barely notice. This is what I'm good at, what I love. The rest of the world falls away, and it's just me and Shakespeare's words on the page.

Or…*not* Shakespeare's words.

That's what I have to prove.

My diploma depends on it.

I start with ambition, of course. Relentless. Almost mindless, really. It deviates from the nuanced character studies that he's known for.

The unflinching gore also stands out. The bloody imagery is more explicit and pervasive than other plays. It lacks the poetic introspection that gives it meaning.

Halfway through, I pause, flexing my cramping fingers.

I glance up, my gaze drifting to the window. The sun is high, casting a warm glow over the campus. It's a beautiful day, a day full of promise.

A day that feels like a beginning, not an end.

I turn back to my essay, a newfound determination burning within me. I'm not just writing for a grade, I'm writing for my future. For the chance to stay and graduate from Tanglewood, to continue exploring the power of words, the magic of literature. For the chance to prove that I belong here, that I deserve this.

Though my pièce de résistance is about the women.

Of course it is.

You liked the stories of strong women, even if Shakespeare didn't give them full thrift. You liked arguing for them, and you're damned good at it.

That's what Ms. O'Connor said to me.

I argue that Lady Macbeth shows more agency than his other female characters. Though less nuance. The same is true of the Weird Sisters. His approach to women is completely different in this play. And though I have no idea who actually wrote *Macbeth*, I know that this difference truly exists.

It's a good argument.

The best final exam paper I've ever written.

Because, as I told Ms. O'Connor, if I don't do it, who will?

I scribble the last sentence, a triumphant flourish of graphite.

I rise from my seat, the legs of the chair scraping against the floor with a satisfying screech. The sound cuts through the hushed whispers and the scratch of pencils on paper, drawing a few glances my way. I ignore them, my focus solely on the blue book in my hand, its pages filled with my thoughts, my arguments, my passion.

I approach Professor Oglevy's desk, the wood worn smooth by years of use. She looks up as I near, her eyes meeting mine over the rim of her glasses. There's a spark in her gaze, a knowing glint that makes my heart skip a beat.

"Finished already, Ms. Hill?" she asks, her voice low, conspiratorial. She leans back in her chair, her fingers drumming a steady rhythm on the desk.

I drop the blue book onto the small stack. "Yes, Professor."

A small smile plays at her lips. "I heard you had your own Italian summer. Perhaps that inspired your writing? We shall see."

My cheeks flush, a warmth spreading across my face. I duck my head, a vain attempt to hide my blush. Though I can't deny the truth of it.

I take a deep breath, filling my lungs with the scent of cut grass and distant rain. It's a smell that promises renewal, growth. A new beginning.

William falls into step beside me, his long legs easily matching my pace. He's quiet for a moment, his hands tucked into the pockets of his jeans. He looks almost like a student, his hair tousled by the wind, his eyes hidden behind a pair of aviators. Almost, but not quite. There's an air of authority about him, a confidence that sets him apart. His shoulders are too broad, his jaw too firm, his strength too tested.

"How did you do?"

I shrug. "I'll find out when I get the grade back."

"Bullshit."

He chuckles, a low rumble that makes me

shiver. "Bullshit."

"Excuse me?"

"You know how you did."

"Fine. It was a good essay. A great one, even."

"Excellent."

"Though why you want me to be full of myself, I don't know."

"It's not full of yourself when it's true. You're the smartest student I've ever met."

My heart melts at his words, a warmth spreading through me. It means more to me than when he calls me beautiful, though I don't mind that, either. I duck my head, trying to hide my blush. "Don't say that kind of thing on campus."

He smirks, a glint in his eyes. "Are you afraid you might swoon?"

I snort. "Hardly."

He leans in, his voice dropping to a low growl. "I could make you swoon, Ms. Hill. Couldn't I? I wouldn't even have to touch that beautiful little body. Wouldn't even have to kiss you. With my words alone, describing what I'll do to you, making you feel, want it, breathe it, I could make you come. Couldn't I?"

I shiver, the heat in his voice sending a wave of desire crashing through me. I can imagine it all too well, the two of us alone, the door locked, the blinds drawn. His hands on my body, his mouth on mine, his voice whispering dirty words in my ear.

I glance around, my cheeks flushing with a heat that has nothing to do with the sun overhead. I've resolved that people will eventually know about our relationship, but that doesn't mean we have to flaunt it.

"Not here," I say, not quite hiding a smile.

"What are they going to do? Put us in the university gossip mill? Fire me from my position? Or perhaps kill me in dramatic fashion?"

I give him a severe look. "Of course not."

William takes my hand, his thumb tracing circles on the back of my hand. His eyes, those deep, intense pools of blue, lock on to mine. "Let them see."

Before I can protest further, he pulls me into his arms, spinning us around in a dizzying twirl. I gasp, my hands clutching his shoulders for support. The world blurs around us, but his face remains clear, his smile wide and ridiculously handsome.

"Come on," he says, setting me down but keeping an arm wrapped around my waist. "Take a selfie. We can send it to Tanglewood Tea."

"You don't even know what a selfie is," I

tease, poking his muscled chest.

"Of course I do. It's a visage made by thine own hand."

A laugh bubbles out of me, a mix of disbelief and joy. "You're old."

He captures my hand, pressing a kiss to my fingertips. "Too old, in fact, for an innocent maiden such as you, but there's no hope for it. I love you, Anne Elizabeth Hill," he says, his voice loud and clear, carrying across the quad.

"Shhh." Except I don't really mean it. He's turned me, studious, serious Anne, into someone who giggles. I don't know how it happened, but I also don't totally hate it. It's fun to be playful with a man, especially when that man is a handsome Shakespeare scholar.

There's a mischievous glint in his eye. "I'd like to say that I don't care who knows it, but that would be a lie. I *do* care. I want every single person on this campus, on every campus, in the entire world, to know that I love you."

My heart swells, threatening to burst out of my chest. I look up at him, this man who has turned my world upside down, who has challenged me, infuriated me, loved me. And I know, in this moment, that I want the world to know it too.

I pull out my phone, holding it up to capture our faces. He presses his cheek against mine, his stubble rough against my skin. I snap the photo, capturing the moment, immortalizing us.

EPILOGUE

Sweet Sorrow

SUNLIGHT BATHES TANGLEWOOD University in a golden glow.

I stand in a sea of black gowns and mortarboards, the cool spring breeze ruffling the tassels that dangle over eager, nervous faces. The air hums with anticipation, a symphony of whispered dreams and barely contained excitement.

I should be exhilarated, triumphant even, but my heart feels heavy, anchored by an absence that gnaws at the edges of my joy. My eyes can't help but scan the crowd for a familiar blonde head, a pair of sparkling blue eyes.

Daisy should be here, her laughter cutting through the tense atmosphere, her hand clutching mine as we navigate this rite of passage together. She wouldn't actually walk in the same ceremony as me, considering our majors. Even this ceremony, containing most of the liberal arts graduates, takes up the entire east lawn.

Daisy should be whooping and hollering in the audience section.

I should be doing the same at her ceremony.

She isn't graduating.

A lump forms in my throat as I look around, the pomp and circumstance suddenly feeling hollow. The grand stage, draped in the university's colors, seems less vibrant without her here to share it with me.

The chatter of proud parents and beaming graduates grates against my ears, a harsh reminder of the silence from Port Lavaca. My parents didn't come—not that I expected them to. I got a congratulations text from Carlisle, though.

To my favorite scholar.

It includes a photo of her lifting a champagne flute. In the background I can see a tumble of backstage equipment, which means she's still in rehearsal for her tour, which made headlines as it sold out. Being supposedly canceled from Tanglewood University did nothing to quell her celebrity. Everyone's dying to see her perform.

I clutch the program in my hands, the paper crinkling under the force of my grip. My name is printed there. It doesn't look quite real, such an ordinary name in an ordinary serif font. Anne

Elizabeth Hill, Magna Cum Laude.

Dean Morris takes the podium. "Graduates, today marks the culmination of your dedication. You studied literature or philosophy or history, but that's not really what matters most. I know, I know, now we tell you." I crack a smile despite my nerves. "The most important skill you acquired here was a love of learning. The most important knowledge you gained was that of human nature—your professors, your fellow students."

He surveys what must be a sea of black hats and gowns.

"The most important power you hold is that of your own understanding. Not what they teach you in books. Not what people tell you to believe. It's your own ability to discern the truth. Today it's both my duty and an honor to preside over this ceremony. Which means I'm sending you all out into a world of clickbait and fake news."

A pause.

"I wish I had a better one, but this is it. Broken and unjust and…beautiful, despite these flaws. You can fix it together. And you will, but it's a large goal. An overwhelming one. So I'll send you off with a smaller one, though just as important.

I'm far away from the stage, the H of Hill being halfway back in the rows, but it looks like a tear glints in his dark eyes. It's confirmed when he becomes choked up.

"Instead of focusing on saving the world," he says, "for now, at the beginning, focus on saving one person. Build a better life, a safer place, a stronger core. For yourself. Because if only one more person in the entire world has that, then you'll have succeeded, even, *especially*, if that person is you."

Tears stream down my face.

I've read many speeches at graduation ceremonies before. It was part of my research, since I have one of my own to give. And apparently my makeup will be ruined by then. I wipe my eyes, smearing whatever light powder I applied. Some speeches exist on a grand scale, encouraging us to be of service, to give generously, to change the world. Other speeches contain more practical, occasionally pithy career advice.

They're all good speeches, but this one…this one feels like it was meant for me.

It's a reminder that I can kill myself trying to save the world.

A reminder that it feels like an impossible task.

Except that I've already done it. I've done it precisely once, when I saved myself. Which means I might be able to do it again, though only if I'm careful. Only if I don't give too much, so much that there's nothing left. Only if I don't lose my way. The world will always need more of me than there even is. It will take and take and take, all for worthy causes. It's up to me to defend my most precious research—myself.

An unconventional send-off perhaps, but one that I needed to hear.

The first row stands, the rustle of gowns and murmurs of excitement filling the air. They begin calling names. I watch as they cross the stage one by one—accepting a scroll from Professor Miller, shaking hands with the dean, moving the tassel from one side to the other. I try to memorize the movements, afraid I'm going to be clumsy in the moment. I'll do them all in the wrong order, and then possibly fall off the stage.

My heart thuds in my chest, a steady drum-beat counting down the moments until it's my turn. I rise on unsteady legs, smoothing down the wrinkles from my gown, the silky fabric rough against my palms. The hat feels too big, perched precariously on my head, the tassel swinging like a pendulum with every movement. Students in front of me ascend the stage. Some of them beam with clear happiness. Others are more subdued, seeming nervous and self-conscious. I'm sure I look terrified.

When they call my name, I climb the steps and cross the stage.

Accept the scroll.

Shake hands.

Professor Miller smiles at me, pride in her hazel eyes.

"Congratulations, Ms. Hill," the dean says, his voice low. "You've earned this."

Move the tassel from one side to the other.

This is a total win. I even manage to take the steps down from the stage without falling on my face. Relief is short-lived. When the other students file back toward our seats, I move to the side. The typical valedictorian's speech is only five to ten minutes long.

However, I'm fairly certain this one's going to last five to ten *years.*

Or at the very least, take that much off my life.

Some small percentage of me wishes that Thorne had stuck around long enough to…well, not to fail me, but maybe a B. That would have brought my GPA down low enough so that I wouldn't have to do this.

Heavy velvet curtains rustle behind me.

A sudden draft sends shivers up the gown.

A strong hand grips my wrist.

Before I can react, it tugs me into the shadows. I stumble, my heart pounding in my chest, as the curtains fall back into place, sealing me off from the noise and the bright lights of the ceremony.

Professor Stratford also wears a gown, though his is made of thicker, more luxurious material, dark green. Instead of the shiny mortarboard, he wears a soft tam in deep red, making up the colors of Tanglewood University. It's an uncomfortable reminder that there's a reason why the Society's dangerous pomp and circumstance once thrived here—there's a touch of it built into the foundation.

William's dark gaze fills with pride and possession. The corners of his mouth lift slightly, a hint of a smile that's both reassuring and alarming. "You're officially not my student anymore. Not a student at all."

"Absolutely not," I whisper, reading his intentions.

"They can't hear us," he murmurs, leaning down to kiss the side of my neck.

The gold honors cord is in the way.

He moves it to kiss my neck, making me shiver. Then he holds the braid in his large hand, brushing a thumb over it in a gesture that makes me flush with memory. It's as if he's caressing it. "Hmm," he says. "It's thinner than the one in the tower, but I think it will still make a very good rope for holding you down."

"Oh my God."

"You seemed nervous. I'm trying to distract you."

"Well, it's working!"

"You've been a very good student."

I swallow hard, my mouth suddenly dry. "Have I?"

His lips curve into a predator's grin that promises both pleasure and pain. "Oh, yes," he says, his fingers tangling in my hair, tilting my head back to expose the column of my throat. "You've learned so much. Now it's time to give you your A."

His mouth descends on mine, a demanding kiss that leaves me gasping. I melt into him, my body pressing against his as his hands roam over my curves, claiming, possessing. His tongue invades my mouth, a sensual assault that leaves me dizzy. I can feel the hard length of him pressing against my belly, a promise of what's to come.

My hands find their way to his chest, my

fingers curling into the soft fabric of his gown. I can feel the steady beat of his heart beneath my palm, a rhythm that matches the pounding of my own. He growls, his hands gripping my hips, holding me tight.

He presses me back against the wall, the rough brick biting into my shoulders. His mouth trails down my neck, his teeth nipping at the sensitive flesh, sending waves of pleasure coursing through me. I arch against him, a moan escaping my lips as his hands cup my breasts, his thumb circling my nipple through the thin fabric.

"You're mine," he says. "Every inch of you belongs to me."

I nod, my breath coming in short gasps. "Yours," I whisper, my voice barely audible.

His mouth captures mine once more, a fierce, possessive kiss that leaves me trembling with need. I can feel the hard length of him pressing against me, the promise of pleasure and pain intertwined. I surrender to him, my body, my soul, my heart. In this moment, there is nothing but him, nothing but us, nothing but the fire that burns between us.

And as his hands slip beneath my skirt, his fingers tracing the edge of my panties, I know that I am lost, utterly and completely.

Lost in him, lost in us, lost in the storm that

rages between us.

There are only a few minutes to put myself together again, to pat my cheeks and straighten my cap before they call my name, again, this time for the speech.

Goddamn it.

I should have taken Advanced Calculus with Daisy.

That definitely would have ruined my GPA.

Instead I climb the stage again and take the podium.

I clear my throat, my hands trembling slightly as I unfold my notes. There's more shifting in the audience, now that everyone has gotten to walk. Or maybe it's only that Dean Morris knows how to command a stage better than me. Students fiddle with the scrolls they've been given. A couple have even taken off their mortarboards, probably itching to throw it into the air.

Five to ten minutes.

Or maybe just an entire lifetime.

"When Dean Morris told me I would have to give this speech, I asked him what it should be about. He said that, now that I'm graduating, I should think independently. So I told him I was opting out of giving a speech. He said…not *that* independently."

Polite laughter. I'll definitely take polite

laughter.

I wrote and rewrote my speech a dozen times, each iteration a struggle to encapsulate my time at Tanglewood University. In the end, I turned to the one thing that always brought me solace, the one thing that always made sense to me—Shakespeare.

Silently, William steps from the wings.

He watches me with pride. And perhaps some worry. I refused to practice it on him, or even show it to him, no matter how much he cajoled.

"I've chosen to deliver my speech in the form of a sonnet," I say, a soft murmur rippling through the audience. "It's a form that's strictly bound by specific metric and rhythmic structure. But within those boundaries, it has power. Within those boundaries, it can change everything. Like our time here at Tanglewood University."

I clear my throat, praying I don't stumble.

"Upon this stage, we stand, our journey's end,
In robes of black, our hearts aflame with
    pride.
Each step we took, each path we chose to
    wend,
Has led us here, where futures wide and bright
    abide."

The words flow from me, a river of emotion that ebbs and surges with each line. I feel the weight of every syllable, the power of every phrase.

> "We laughed, we cried, we fought, we loved, we lost,
> In hallowed halls and shadows cast by moon.
> Each moment shared, each memory embossed,
> A tapestry of youth, forever strewn."

This is my story, our story, the tale of a thousand dreams and a million heartaches, of triumphs and failures, of love and loss. This is graduation.

> "So let us stand, on this our graduation,
> Not as the end, but as a new creation.
> For we are Tanglewood, and we shall be,
> Forever bound, in love and memory."

When I finish the last word, the crowd is silent. I would wonder if I even said the words, except that I feel them resound in my chest. And then a roar hits me—clapping, shouting. Tears shine in eyes. Some of these people I know. Others I don't. In this moment, we're together. We're united. We're throwing our mortarboards into the sky, apparently, a smattering of black caps soaring across pale blue.

I take off my own and toss it into the air. It goes diagonal, of course. I've never been into sports. So it's lost in a sea of people, but it doesn't matter. Now when Dean Morris is there to shake my hand again, to squeeze my shoulder, before sending me, gently, into William's waiting arms beside the stage.

Which is good. I wouldn't have been able to navigate the stairs, not with tears flooding my eyes. This is not goodbye. It's a beginning, a promise of things to come. This is Tanglewood, and we shall be, forever bound, in love and memory.

As the applause continues, I step back from the podium, my heart full, my spirit soaring. The future stretches out before me, a blank page waiting to be filled. And I am ready, pen in hand, to write the next chapter of my story.

Then it's William's turn.

Stratford's gaze sweeps across the crowd, his eyes lingering on mine for a moment that feels like an eternity. A shiver runs down my spine, a mix of excitement and trepidation. This is it—the end of our journey, the beginning of something new.

"Ladies and gentlemen," he begins, his voice

deep and commanding, resonating through the auditorium like a symphony. "Today, we gather here to celebrate the achievements of these remarkable individuals, to honor their dedication, their perseverance, and their unyielding pursuit of knowledge."

His words wash over me, a soothing balm that calms the storm raging within. I can feel the weight of his gaze, the unspoken promises that hang in the air between us. The future is uncertain, a vast expanse of unknowns and possibilities. But in this moment, there is only him—only us.

"As I stand before you today," he continues, his voice steady and sure, "I am reminded of the words of the Bard himself. 'Parting is such sweet sorrow.' And indeed, it is with a heavy heart that I bid you all farewell."

A collective sigh ripples through the audience, a shared sense of loss and longing. Tanglewood has been our home, our sanctuary, our battleground. It has shaped us, molded us, forged us into the people we are today. And now, it is time to say goodbye.

"But," Stratford says, a smile tugging at the corners of his mouth, "as we part ways, let us not forget the lessons we have learned, the friendships we have forged, the love we have found. Let us carry these memories with us, a beacon of light to guide us through the darkest nights."

His eyes find mine once more, a silent communication that speaks volumes. My heart swells with emotion, a mix of joy and sorrow, of hope and fear. This is our moment, our farewell—and I am determined to make the most of it.

"And so," he concludes, his voice barely above a whisper, "I leave you with one final thought. 'Love all, trust a few, do wrong to none.' May your paths be filled with love, with trust, with righteousness. And may you always, always find your way back home."

The auditorium erupts in applause, a thunderous ovation that fills the room and reverberates through my very soul. I can feel the tears welling up in my eyes, the lump forming in my throat. This is it—the end of an era, the beginning of something new.

And then, without warning, Stratford steps away from the podium, his eyes locked on to mine. He crosses the stage in three long strides, his movements fluid and sure. The auditorium falls silent, the air thick with anticipation. I can feel the weight of a thousand eyes upon us, the collective intake of breath.

He reaches me, his hands cupping my face, his

thumbs brushing away the tears that streak my cheeks. His eyes are a storm of emotion, a swirling vortex of desire and longing and love. I can see the future reflected in their depths, a future filled with promise, with possibility, with us.

And then, he kisses me.

It is a kiss that steals my breath away, a kiss that sets my soul on fire. His lips are soft and firm, his taste a heady mix of mint and man. I melt into him, my body pressing against his, my hands gripping the lapels of his suit. The world around us fades away, the applause, the cheers, the expectant faces. There is only him, only me, only us.

The kiss deepens, his tongue invading my mouth, a sensual assault that leaves me gasping for breath. I can feel the heat radiating from his body, the subtle shift of his muscles beneath his suit. His hands tangle in my hair, tilting my head back to expose the column of my throat. His mouth trails down my neck, his teeth nipping at the sensitive flesh, sending waves of pleasure coursing through me.

The auditorium erupts in cheers, a roar of approval that fills the room and reverberates through my very soul. I can hear the whistles, the catcalls, the shouts of encouragement. But it is all a distant hum, a background noise to the symphony that plays within me.

And then, as suddenly as it began, the kiss ends. Stratford pulls away, his breath coming in short gasps, his eyes burning into mine. I can see the future reflected in their depths, a future filled with promise, with possibility, with us.

"I love you," he whispers, his voice barely audible. "I have always loved you. And I will love you, forever and always."

The tears spill over, streaming down my cheeks in a torrent of emotion. I can feel the weight of his words, the power of his love. It is a love that transcends time, that defies convention, that conquers all.

And in that moment, I know—this is not the end. This is not a goodbye. This is a beginning, a promise of things to come. This is Tanglewood, and we shall be, forever bound, in love and memory.

As the applause continues, I stand there, my heart full, my spirit soaring. The future stretches out before me, a blank page waiting to be filled. And I am ready, pen in hand, to write the next chapter of my story.

Thank you for reading THE FINAL EXAM! Want more Professor Stratford and Anne? You can read a steamy bonus epilogue from when they visit the theater in London where Shakespeare staged his plays. Download bonus epilogue now> www.skyewarren.com/bonus=university

Want to read Dean Blake Morris's story?

Once upon a time there was a beautiful college student…

And a beastly professor with scars he can't hide.

Erin cleans Mr. Morris's house twice a week to pay her tuition. The reclusive ex-soldier intimidates her, but she can't help but feel sympathy for him. Then she walks in on him touching himself…and moaning her name. The flames scorch them both, but she never expected him to be the professor on the first day of the semester.

Professor Avery Miller also has a story set in Tanglewood!

The price of survival...

Gabriel Miller swept into my life like a storm. He tore down my father with cold retribution, leaving him penniless in a hospital bed. I quit my private all-girls college to take care of the only family I have left.

There's one way to save our house, one thing I have left of value.

My virginity.

A forbidden auction...

Gabriel appears at every turn. He seems to take pleasure in watching me fall. Other times he's the only kindness in a brutal underworld.

Except he's playing a deeper game than I know. Every move brings us together, every secret rips us apart. And when the final piece is played, only one of us can be left standing.

"Sinfully sexy and darkly beautiful, The Pawn will play games with your heart and leave you craving more!"

—Laura Kaye, New York Times
bestselling author

Sign up for the VIP Reader List to get free books, bonus scenes, and find out when my books go on sale: www.skyewarren.com/newsletter

I appreciate your help in spreading the word, including telling a friend. Reviews help readers find books! Please leave a review on your favorite book site.

You can also join my Facebook group, Skye Warren's Dark Room, for exclusive giveaways and sneak peeks of future books.

Keep reading for an excerpt from THE PAWN…

ONE THICK EYEBROW rises. "What do you want with him?"

A sense of familiarity fills the space between us even though I know we haven't met. This man is a stranger, but he looks at me as if he wants to know me. He looks at me as if he already does. There's an intensity to his eyes when they sweep over my face, as firm and as telling as a touch.

"I need…" My heart thuds as I think about all the things I need—a rewind button. One person in the city who doesn't hate me by name alone. "I need a loan."

He gives me a slow perusal, from the nervous

slide of my tongue along my lips to the high neckline of my clothes. I tried to dress professionally—a black cowl-necked sweater and pencil skirt. His strange amber gaze unbuttons my coat, pulls away the expensive cotton, tears off the fabric of my bra and panties. He sees right through me, and I shiver as a ripple of awareness runs over my skin.

I've met a million men in my life. Shaken hands. Smiled. I've never felt as seen through as I do right now. Never felt like someone has turned me inside out, every dark secret exposed to the harsh light. He sees my weaknesses, and from the cruel set of his mouth, he likes them.

His lids lower. "And what do you have for collateral?"

Nothing except my word. That wouldn't be worth anything if he knew my name. I swallow past the lump in my throat. "I don't know."

Nothing.

He takes a step forward, and suddenly I'm crowded against the brick wall beside the door, his large body blocking out the warm light from inside. He feels like a furnace in front of me, the heat of him in sharp contrast to the cold brick at my back. "What's your name, girl?"

The word *girl* is a slap in the face. I force

myself not to flinch, but it's hard. Everything about him overwhelms me—his size, his low voice. "I'll tell Mr. Scott my name."

In the shadowed space between us, his smile spreads, white and taunting. The pleasure that lights his strange yellow eyes is almost sensual, as if I caressed him. "You'll have to get past me."

My heart thuds. He likes that I'm challenging him, and God, that's even worse. What if I've already failed? I'm free-falling, tumbling, turning over without a single hope to anchor me. Where will I go if he turns me away? What will happen to my father?

"Let me go," I whisper, but my hope fades fast.

His eyes flash with warning. "Little Avery James, all grown up."

A small gasp resounds in the space between us. He already knows my name. That means he knows who my father is. He knows what he's done. Denials rush to my throat, pleas for understanding. The hard set of his eyes, the broad strength of his shoulders tells me I won't find any mercy here.

Want to read more? Find THE PAWN at Amazon, Apple Books, and other bookstores!

Books by Skye Warren

Endgame Trilogy & more books in Tanglewood
The Pawn
The Knight
The Castle
The King
The Queen
The CEO
The Heiress
The Player
The Escort
The Bishop

North Security Trilogy & more North brothers
Overture
Concerto
Sonata
Audition
Diamond in the Rough
Gold Mine
Silver Lining
Finale

Rochester Trilogy & more
Private Property
Strict Confidence
Best Kept Secret
Hiding Places
Behind Closed Doors

Stripped series
Tough Love
Love the Way You Lie
Better When It Hurts
Even Better
Pretty When You Cry
Caught for Christmas
Hold You Against Me
To the Ends of the Earth

The Modern Fairy Tale Duet
Beauty and the Professor
Falling for the Beast

**For a complete listing of Skye Warren books,
visit
www.skyewarren.com/books**

About the Author

Skye Warren is the bestselling author of dangerous romance such as the Endgame trilogy. Her books have been on the New York Times, the USA Today, and the Wall Street Journal bestseller lists. They feature powerful men and the strong women who bring them to their knees. She makes her home in Texas with her loving family and her many, many dogs.

Sign up for Skye's newsletter:
skyewarren.com/newsletter

Like Skye Warren on Facebook:
facebook.com/skyewarren

Join Skye Warren's Dark Room reader group:
skyewarren.com/darkroom

Follow Skye Warren on Instagram:
instagram.com/skyewarrenbooks

Visit Skye's website for her current booklist:
skyewarren.com/books

Copyright

This is a work of fiction. Any resemblance to actual persons, living or dead, business establishments, events or locales is entirely coincidental. All rights reserved. Except for use in a review, the reproduction or use of this work in any part is forbidden without the express written permission of the author.

The Final Exam © 2024 by Skye Warren
Print Edition

Formatting by BB eBooks
Cover by Book Beautiful
Proofreading by Judy's Proofreading & Sisters Get Lit.erary